THE BILLIONAIRE'S RETREAT

RACHEL HANNA

CHAPTER 1

15 Years Previous

She stood on the edge of the old bridge and stared down at the deep ravine below. One second. That's all it would take, and this nightmare of a life she'd been living would be over.

She wondered what came next. Once she fell, would it be painful? Or would everything just go black? Would she even know she'd died? Would all of those life after death stories she'd heard be true? Would she see her beloved grandmother or the fish she'd had in elementary school? But her biggest question was whether she'd find peace wherever she was going.

Jill Russell wasn't a dummy. She knew what her preacher had said about suicide on Sunday mornings when he'd warned that those who took their own lives would end up in hell for all eternity, but was that really true?

Her fifteen year old mind couldn't comprehend a God that wouldn't understand how miserable her current existence was. And no matter how much she'd prayed in recent months, things were going from bad to worse.

Her new step father was a horrible man, intent on making her feel so small and ugly and stupid. Her mother ignored her most of the time now, opting instead to focus her attentions on the new baby she'd made with that monster she called a husband. And while she loved her baby sister, she knew she'd never measure up again.

And then there was the constant bullying. The kids at her new school, the third one in as many years, pick on her relentlessly about things she couldn't control. Her second hand clothes. Her "spooky" eyes. The smattering of freckles on her nose.

No one wanted her. No one loved her. And therefore, life was pointless. It'd be better for everyone if she'd just take that one step over the edge...

"Hey!" she heard a male voice say from the other end of the rickety old bridge. She could barely see him because of the bright sun. Maybe she'd already jumped and he was her spirit guide? Otherwise, why would anyone else be so far out in the woods?

She had been forced to come camping with her family even though her mother knew she hated being outdoors. With fair skin and red tinged hair, the sun wasn't her friend.

"I said hey! Can you hear me?" the guy said as he walked closer. She got scared for a split second, but then realized if he was an axe murderer, she could just jump because either way she ended up in the same place.

"What?" she finally said, irritated that this guy was interrupting her dramatic plan to end her suffering. Who was he to force her to have a conversation anyway?

"What are you doing up here?" He was carefully looking down at the wooden slats as he walked. The bridge was in horrible shape and obviously not used anymore. It didn't even seem to be attached to a road. It was just randomly out in the woods, a literal road going nowhere.

"What business is it of yours?" she asked, stepping back a bit. As he got closer, she realized he had to be close to her age.

The guy stopped and looked at her as if he was slowly taking in the whole scene and realizing what was actually going on. She felt almost naked in front of him as he eyed her up and down.

"Were you about to jump?"

She pursed her lips. "Maybe."

"Are you crazy?"

She laughed. "Well, I would assume so since throwing myself off this crappy bridge seems like the best idea I've had in awhile."

"I'm Jesse."

"So?"

"And you are?"

"None of your business." She sighed and sat down cross legged a few feet from the edge. This guy was really getting on her nerves.

"Oh, come on. It's not like I'm going to look you up and stalk you or something." He sat down beside her with a couple of feet between them.

He wasn't a bad looking guy, as far as teenage boys went. He had thick, medium brown hair that fell almost to his shoulders and a little stubble starting to form on his upper lip.

"Fine. My name is Jill."

"So, what's up, Jill?" he said, leaning back on his arms like they were just having a normal conversation.

"Look, if you're trying to stop me from jumping, it's not

going to work. If I want to jump, I'll just jump. And if you try to stop me, I'll take you with me."

He chuckled. "Listen, my life sucks too, but I don't want to jump because I have tickets to a baseball game in a few weeks. So, if you wanna jump, go right ahead. Nobody here's going to stop you."

Jill was shocked. What kind of guy tells a girl to jump if she wants? What the heck? She was a stranger to him, but still, where was the human decency?

"Wow, you're quite a nice guy," she said, irritated.

"What?"

"You tell a girl to jump if she wants?"

"Well, if I asked you not to jump, would it matter?"

She turned and stared straight out into the massive forest. "No."

"So why should I bother?"

She twisted her head back toward him. "Because it's the *kind* thing to do. You know, help someone."

"Do you need help, Jill?" he asked softly.

Her eyes threatened to well up with tears, but she refused to give this guy the satisfaction.

"Not anymore."

"So what's so bad in your life that you're willing to end it all anyway?"

"None of your business."

He chuckled. "Come on. I'm curious."

"What, are you writing a book or something? Just leave me alone."

She could hear thunder starting to rumble in the distance. It was becoming more and more overcast. Maybe this guy would scurry off to his campsite once the rain started, and she could just get this over with.

"Nah, I'm not much of a writer. Failed English last year."

"My Mom would kill me if I failed a class," she said. Her Mom. Talking about her made her heart ache. Why didn't her own mother love her anymore?

"Yeah? Well, that must mean she cares, right?"

"Only because she doesn't want to pay for college one day. She says I have to get scholarships, or I won't be going to college."

"Are you planning to go to college?"

"I was thinking about it... Wait! Stop trying to trip me up, Jesse." She crossed her arms and turned back toward the ravine below.

"Hmmm.... Seems to me that a girl thinking of jumping off a bridge may not be so sure if she's also thinking about college."

She sighed and laid back against the warm wooden slats, her legs now dangling precariously over the edge.

"What do you think happens when you die?" she asked. Jesse laid back beside her, both of them staring up at the gray sky.

"I don't know. I think there's a heaven, I guess."

"I hope so," she said softly.

He paused for a few moments. "I think life is a series of tests."

"Tests?" she asked, turning her head toward him. He actually looked kind of cute laying down.

"Yeah. Like we're in some kind of video game, ya know? Obstacles... like maybe fireballs and dynamite... keep getting thrown our way. And we like dodge and weave and roll, trying to avoid them. Sometimes, we get hit. Sometimes, we don't. But each one teaches us how to get stronger and faster, right? So then when we're like old and gray, we sort of graduate... up to heaven."

Jill giggled. "That's quite a theory you've come up with."

"Well, I figure it's better than the theory that life just sucks and won't ever get better, right?"

She turned back and stared at the sky. "Maybe it doesn't ever get better, Jesse."

"I once knew this kid in school whose mom and step dad both died within three months of each other. He ended up in foster care. Went to six different houses, some of them really bad. One of the dads beat him pretty good."

"Why are you telling me this?"

"Because that boy kept trying, Jill. He didn't give up, even when he came to school with a black eye sometimes."

"What happened to him?"

Jesse smiled. "He's laying right here beside you."

She sat up slowly and turned to face him. "They beat you up?" Jesse sat up too.

He smiled slightly. "Yeah."

Instinctively, she reached out and touched his face. "Here?"

"Among other places."

Her hand lingered on his cheek for a moment until he reached up and held it in his. "It's never bad enough to give up the one life you have, Jill. Never."

"Maybe you're just stronger than I am."

Jesse smiled again. "I doubt that. You seem pretty tough."

She sighed. "I don't know how to live like this."

"It's tough, I get it. But you're what, fifteen?"

"Good guess."

"Not much longer, and you can be on your own. Spend time planning for your future, Jill. Nobody can take your dreams from you."

Just then, droplets of rain started to fall, first lightly but then harder and harder.

"Oh crap!" Jill said, giggling as they both stood up. Jesse

took hold of her arm, pulling her away from the edge. To be honest, she felt relieved to be away from the view of the abyss below.

Laughing, they ran to an overhang at the edge of the bridge and huddled together.

"Guess I should've checked the weather!" Jesse yelled over the loud downpour.

"Guess I should've planned my death better," she said back with a laugh. His eyes went serious.

"Please tell me you won't do this, Jill." He put his hands on her arms and stared into her eyes. "Wow."

"What?"

"I didn't realize the color of your eyes."

"Yeah, they're awful. This weird blue color. They call me spooky at school."

He stared at her for an uncomfortably long moment. "No, they're beautiful. Don't listen to bullies because they lie. They're jealous."

She smiled. "You're just being nice."

"No. I'm not even that nice. Trust me. I'm being honest."

Jill couldn't help but smile. "Thanks."

"I need to go, but I'm not leaving here until you leave too."

"How do you know I won't come back here?" she asked.

"Because you're going to promise me that you won't."

"And why would I do that?" she asked, crossing her arms.

"Because of this," he said softly before pressing his lips to hers. It was only a brief moment in time, but to Jill it felt like her whole world flipped upside down in that moment. She'd never been kissed before, and if kissing was like this with everyone, she didn't understand why people weren't kissing like this all day every day.

When he pulled back, he smiled down at her.

"Why did you do that?" she asked.

"To give you something to live for. Maybe one day we'll meet again," he said, taking her hand and leading her off the bridge, the rain pelting them the whole way. When they got to the other side, they stood there looking at each other for a moment. "Promise me."

"I promise," she said softly. And with that, Jesse kissed her cheek and ran off into the woods, like a figment of her imagination.

～

Present Day

Patrick stood in his office overlooking Atlanta and let out the sharp breath he'd been holding.

"Look, Don, I'm not budging even a millimeter on this. Either you guys sign the papers today, or we're walking. I've got opportunities all over this state, so replacing this deal could literally be done over lunch. You got me?"

As he listened, he ran his fingers through his hair, a sure sign that he needed to pop another blood pressure pill. Stress was not his friend, even at just thirty years old. His doctor was worried every time he had a check up.

"Have the papers in my email in thirty minutes. Otherwise, we're done." He pressed end on his cell phone and flung it behind him onto the desk.

Sometimes, being the boss sucked. But he was more than the boss. He was the owner, and that often sucked even more.

Being the only billionaire he knew meant he was at the very top of the food chain, so to speak, so getting any real advice from a mentor was out of the question. In reality,

Patrick had never thought he'd become an actual billionaire. He hadn't even tried to become one. He had just wanted to be successful. To never hurt for money. To be comfortable. And he was. Financially, at least.

He tried not to think about the fact that he hadn't been in a stable relationship in three years. Or the fact that his family consisted of him and him alone. Or the concerns his doctor had about his current health.

"You've got to relax," the doc would say every time he came in for a visit. Usually he was there for a migraine or neck pain, always the result of the major stress he was under. And truthfully, he'd always assumed rich people didn't have these problems. Maybe he'd thought that the super wealthy didn't get headaches, but that was far from the truth. While he no longer worried about his bills, he sure as heck had problems just like anyone else.

His meteoric rise in the real estate business had far exceeded what anyone thought he could do, including him. But when he'd helped to invent some new commercial real estate software and the coordinating app to go with it, his bank account had fattened up faster than he could've imagined. He'd never seen so many zeroes in his life.

Now, as the owner of a massive real estate company, Patrick was under more stress than ever. And this current week was the busiest he'd had in awhile.

"Excuse me, sir?" The newest intern was standing in his doorway, a file folder clutched tight against her chest. She looked terrified.

"Yes?"

"Mr. James asked me to bring this to you. It's the file on the mountain property," she said, her voice shaky. Sometimes he wondered why the local college sent these types of people to work at his company. She looked scared of her own shadow.

"Okay," he said, walking toward her. "And you are?"

She giggled. "Oh, sorry. I'm Amy. I just started this morning."

"Right," he said, not making eye contact. "Good luck."

He turned back toward his desk. She lingered there for a moment before walking back down the hall. He hated not to be friendly, but he just didn't have time. Making friends, or even acquaintances, that didn't lead to more income was pointless.

As he sat back down at his desk and opened the file, he steeled himself for yet another deal that he'd probably pass on. The banks often sent him potential deals, usually companies that were about to go under, and he could swallow them up before the bank ever had to lose a penny.

But the mountains? No thanks. He hadn't been up that way in years. He wasn't exactly a mountain man. He preferred city properties. Skyscrapers. Big industrial parks. He'd spent plenty of time in those blue tinged mountains as a kid, and he didn't plan to ever go back there.

As he opened the folder and started looking at the paperwork inside, Patrick was struck. He knew this property. He knew it very well.

Surprisingly, his hands started to shake a bit as he looked at the photos. This was a place he'd let go of in his mind a long time ago. Things had happened there. Some good, some bad. His stomach churned as he thought about it. What were the odds this file would land on his desk?

After popping an antacid, his third one of the morning, he picked up his cell and dialed the number for his contact at the bank.

"Jim? Yeah, this is Patrick. Listen, I really can't go to this mountain property, man... Why? Well, I'm more of a city guy... I know, I know. It would be perfect for the conference center project... Okay, you're right. This deal is too good to pass up. I'll head up there this weekend. Thanks."

Patrick ended the call and stared down at the pile of pictures on his desk. Never in a million years had he expected to go back there. At least this time, the two people he never wanted to see again wouldn't be there. Just the memories. The good ones and the bad ones.

CHAPTER 2

Jill stood there, arms opened wide, her eyes closed. "Deep breath in, hold for a count of four... One... Two... Three.... Four... And then let it out slowly, for a count of seven... And again, deep breath in..."

She'd said this same thing over and over again for the last three years. Every class was different, filled with people who had come to her retreat to learn how to de-stress and relax. Type A business people, mothers who'd lost children, service members with PTSD... They'd all flocked there at first, her reputation for helping to heal their anxiety and depression spreading like wildfire around the area and beyond.

But she'd known from the outset that buying this place and sinking every dime she had into it was risky. And now, she had no idea how to soothe her own anxious thoughts. It was never a good thing to open the mail and see pink papers in every envelope. She could hear time ticking away inside her head every single day, and there didn't seem to be a dang thing she could do about it.

The Retreat was about to be no more.

When she'd taken the leap into being an entrepreneur three years ago, she'd had on rose colored glasses, for sure. A lot of her friends had tried to talk her down. They'd told her to take it slow, not take out so many loans, scale down her plans.

But Jill had felt an urge, a calling, to lead people out of the darkness. She'd spent years toiling away as a waitress, saving every dime she made to go toward her dream. No one else was going to help her, after all. She didn't talk to her family anymore, hadn't in years. And sometimes she felt like a big fake, standing in front of all these people, proclaiming she had the answers to inner peace. She wasn't feeling at all peaceful right now.

"Now, sweep your arms over your head and stretch toward the sky, like a flower opening itself to the sun..." she said in her best soothing voice. It was the same script mostly, which made it easy enough to get through even on days when she wasn't feeling herself. And today was definitely one of those days.

An early morning call from her mortgage holder - which had interrupted her own meditation - had rocked her sense of calm like a lightning bolt. They were foreclosing. She had no more "stays of execution," so to speak. Pretty soon, she'd be forced to walk up to the edge of the plank and jump off into the deep watery abyss.

Okay, maybe she was being just a bit dramatic. But that's what it felt like.

She had no plan B. No family to run back to. No boyfriend or husband to hold her and tell her everything was going to be all right.

When she'd bought this place and poured her heart and

soul into it, never in her wildest nightmares had there been even a thought in the back of her mind that she'd one day lose it all. But she was dangerously close to that happening.

When her lender had told her an investor was coming to take a look at an adjacent property and they wanted her to let him see The Retreat at the same time, her stomach had churned. The conversation rang in her head even now.

"I don't understand. I haven't been foreclosed. This is still my property!"

"That's technically true, but you're behind several months now, and we've been more than lenient, Miss Russell. I think we both know what the outcome of this is going to be..."

"Mr. Randall, you've underestimated me," she'd said, fully unsure of where she was going with this. "I'm not going to lose my business."

He cleared his throat. "I hope you're right. But this gentleman is buying up all the surrounding property for a conference center and resort. Your property stands firmly in the middle of all that, so he needs to see it."

"You can't force me to allow this," she said, feeling fairly certain she was right legally.

He sighed so loud she had to pull the phone from her ear. "Maybe that's true. But we've been very *lenient* with you," he repeated. "And that can be revoked at any time."

She pursed her lips and struggled to keep calm. "Is that a threat?"

"No. It's just a fact, Miss Russell. If we need to speed up the process of foreclosure, we're well within our rights to do so. Or, as we'd prefer, you can keep running your business until such time as the other property sells."

"Or until I save my property."

He paused. "Right. I suppose that's another possibility."

She could almost hear laughter breaking through in his voice. A tear rolled down her cheek, and she wasn't someone who cried often. She wiped it away almost violently and hung up the phone.

"How long should we keep holding up our arms?" An older woman asked, her arms shaking above her head.

Jill felt terrible that she'd let her mind wander. "I'm so sorry, Agnes. Bring your arms down, sweeping them to your sides..." she said, bringing her focus back to her class. "Okay, that's all for this morning's session. I'll see you guys back here before dinner!"

She made her way into the small office off the pavilion where she taught her classes and quickly shut the door. Normally, she spent time chatting with her guests after class, but her nerves were so frayed that she didn't want to give up the appearance of having it all together.

After all, it was part of her persona and had been since she was a kid. Never let them see you sweat. Strength above all else. Until one day when she'd allowed the darkness in her mind to break through.

It was a brief moment in time, but it had almost destroyed her. She didn't like to think about that day.

Plus, she was pretty sure she would burst into tears at any provocation right now, and that didn't exactly inspire repeat business to see the owner have a nervous breakdown.

"Hey. Are you okay?"

She turned to see her assistant, Kaylee, standing in the doorway. She was a young woman, college age, who had offered to take a job at The Retreat for practically nothing right after it opened. Kaylee wanted to own a yoga practice one day and considered The Retreat to be the best place to get training for her own dreams.

"I'm fine. Just a little tired today."

Kaylee looked at her carefully, her big brown eyes staring through Jill. "You seem more than tired."

"Don't worry about me," Jill said, walking forward and rubbing her arm. "Why are you still here anyway?"

Kaylee swallowed hard. "I don't know how to tell you this."

Jill nodded her head and smiled sadly. "You're leaving me, aren't you?"

Kaylee's big eyes were now filled with tears, her thick, dark lashes doing their best to stop the stream of droplets that started to fall. Jill brushed one away with her thumb. She didn't have children of her own, as much as she wanted them, so Kaylee was the next best thing.

"I'm so sorry. It's just, I got my apartment and I'm barely making rent..."

"Because I haven't been able to pay you on time lately," Jill said quietly. The shame in her body was almost overwhelming. Her failures were now seeping into this poor girl's life.

"It's not your fault..." Kaylee said between sobs. "I love it here, but I just can't..."

Jill put her hands on Kaylee's shoulders and smiled. "I totally understand, sweetie. And it's time for you to move on and start your life. You're so talented! And you're always welcome here."

Would there even be a "here" in a few weeks or months?

After calming Kaylee down and saying her goodbyes, Jill sat down at her small, second hand desk and stared out the window at the forest surrounding her. She felt as alone as she ever had in her life. This place held a part of her soul. How would she ever give it up?

~

Patrick parked his rental, a sexy little sports car, at the end of the long and winding gravel driveway. He hadn't remembered the terrain being so steep, but he was a kid at the time and not exactly paying attention to those sorts of things. After all, he was under a bit of duress back then. Shaking his head to rid it of the memories that were already creeping back into his brain, he walked around the car, inspecting it for any dings that were caused by it being pelted with rocks.

Of course, he was a wealthy man. One of the wealthiest in the world, most likely. So he didn't exactly have to worry about such things. But old habits die hard, and money was a newer part of his life. Not only hadn't he grown up with a silver spoon in his mouth, he regularly went without food at all. For days sometimes. He shook his head again and grumbled,

"Let it go," he said to himself as he looked up at the big, log building. It was more rustic than he'd thought it would be, but what could one expect when it was called The Retreat. It definitely wasn't the Ritz.

He walked toward the steep front steps and stared up at it. His bank contact had told him this woman wasn't going to be happy about his presence. But, from the sounds of it, she didn't have much choice in the matter. People who didn't pay their bills on time shouldn't get a say so, in his opinion. Money was money. Emotions couldn't get involved.

He knocked on the door and waited, but no one came. After a few moments, he hesitantly opened it. This was the South, and guns were commonplace. The last thing he wanted was a big gunshot hole in his new Italian suit.

The place looked empty, even though there were cars in the driveway. He called out, but no one answered.

"Hello?" he called again as he made his way to the back

of the building. Still no answer. Just as he was about to give up and go call his contact, he heard a faint voice. He followed the sound. It was a woman's voice, likely the owner. Realizing she was on the other side of a door, he stopped short, waiting for her to come out.

"I know, Nina. But this is my home. My business. You know how much I love this place and the people I get to help."

He couldn't help but overhear her. But Patrick Scott didn't do emotions. They were a sign of weakness, and he was anything but weak. In the business world, weakness got you smashed under another person's expensive leather dress shoes.

He cleared his throat loudly.

"I think someone's here. I'll call you back," she said, hurriedly. Moments later, the door swung open and they were face to face.

She was wearing yoga pants and a tight fitting gray t-shirt. But when his eyes met hers, he struggled to keep it together. Those eyes. He could never forget them.

Her face searched his for a moment. "Can I help you?"

She didn't remember him. Of course, he was a kid back then. Shaggy hair covered half his face. He was skinnier. Scrawny. Not toned and muscular like he was now. And his hair had darkened over the years.

"I'm Patrick Scott. I think the bank told you I was coming?"

Her face fell. There was puffiness beneath her eyes, obviously from extensive periods of crying. And then he noticed those pouty lips that he'd kissed all those years ago. He tried not to think about it.

"Oh. Yes. Well, you'll excuse me if I don't welcome you,

Mr. Scott. I'm not exactly thrilled to have you here," she said as she walked past him.

Shocked, he turned and followed her. She was fast for such a petite woman.

"Excuse me?"

"You're trying to steal my business right out from under me!" she said, whirling around and almost tripping him in the process.

He sighed. "Look, this is business. You can't be emotional about it."

Her eyebrows furrowed together tightly. "You're kidding me, right?" She put her hands on her hips and glared at him.

"No, I'm not."

"Wow. You must be fun to live with," she said, turning and walking again. Where was she going?

He followed behind her. "I don't actually live with anyone."

She stopped again. He had to quit following her so closely because that time almost resulted in a collision.

"Surprise, surprise. A man with no emotion definitely shouldn't have a wife or girlfriend. She'd be miserable."

The comment hit him harder than he wanted to admit. This woman was tough. How she'd gotten herself into this financial mess was a mystery to him. And he wasn't going to care. He had to separate that one small memory from his adolescence with what was happening now.

She turned and started walking again. "Where are you going?"

"I have a business to run, Mr. Scott."

He walked behind her until she stopped at a coffee station on wheels. She messed with the little machine as if it was a ritual, putting teacups and saucers out on a table. She had a variety of tea bags, an electric tea kettle and some kind of little cookie things he couldn't identify.

"What are those?" he asked, curiosity getting the better of him.

She turned and rolled her eyes. "They are date cookies with raw almonds and cinnamon."

"Yuck," he said under his breath.

She smiled slightly. "Not a healthy eater?"

"I'm not a granola crunching vegan, if that's what you mean. But I eat a salad here and there."

"Try one." She held the cookie out on a small napkin.

"No."

"Try one."

"No."

"Mr. Scott, you might actually steal this place away from me. The least you could do is try one of my very popular cookies."

"Cookies have chocolate chips. Not dates."

"Try it."

He sighed. "Fine." He took the round, dark thing and popped it into his mouth.

"Well?"

"It's not awful."

She laughed. "I'll consider that high praise coming from you."

Feeling that her shell might be cracking a little, Patrick spoke. "Look, Jill..."

"How did you know my name?"

He froze for the first time in years. Crap. She couldn't know who he was. It would only complicate things and make her think there was hope to save her place.

"I, um, saw it on your business card. When I walked

through here. On that table over there." He pointed across the room, hoping that the cards he saw were actually hers and not some date supplier or guru friend.

She looked at the table and then back at him. "Oh."

"As I was saying... I don't want this to be stressful for you. I'm sure it's difficult to come to terms with losing your business. It happens to a lot of people..."

"Stop," she said, holding up her hand. "First off, I have no intention of losing my business. Secondly, that rehearsed little story of yours might come off as more believable if you had any inkling of emotion on your face while you said it."

"Excuse me?"

She walked closer to him, making him completely uncomfortable in the process. Not many people had that affect on him.

"You're detached, Mr. Scott," she said softly, looking up at him. Those eyes really were something. He stiffened and jutted out his chin.

"You don't know me."

"Oh, I know you very well."

"What?" Now his hands were getting sweaty. She recognized him?

"I know your type. All stiff and business-like. No wife. No girlfriend. All work and no play. You know what happens to people like that?"

He cleared his throat. "What?"

"They die young." She stepped back and crossed her arms.

"Okay, look, I'm not here to get psychoanalyzed by a yoga teacher."

"Yoga teacher? Is that what you think I am?" She put her hands on her hips again, causing him to look down and notice her body. She was petite, but she still had curves in all the right places.

"Well, in that you do teach yoga here..."

She chuckled. "Yes, I do teach yoga. But there's a lot more that happens here at The Retreat, Mr. Scott."

"Please call me Patrick."

"Okay, Patrick... we don't just teach yoga classes here. This place changes lives."

"Whatever. I'm here to assess this property and all that is currently on it. I need to start making plans on what to salvage, what to tear down..."

"Tear down? Are you serious? This building isn't even four years old!"

"Progress sometimes requires tearing things down, Jill."

"Miss Russell."

Patrick smiled. "Fine. Miss Russell."

"This is exhausting. What do you want from me?"

"Well, first, it'd be nice if you could show me around this building and any other buildings you have. There's a possibility we could make use of them in our conference center project, even if they just become storage areas."

"Storage? Dear God."

"I know this is hard..."

"Please," she said, holding up her hand again. "No more rehearsed speeches. Just know this; I won't go down without a fight. This place is in my blood. I've poured everything I have into it, and I love it like it's my child. So please don't mistake my kindness of showing you around as weakness. I don't intend to go anywhere."

Her eyes pierced right through him. A part of him wanted to reach out, touch her cheek, see if her skin still felt the same. As much as he hated to admit it, no one else in his life had ever made such an impact after such a brief encounter. He'd never forgotten her. He'd wondered about her for years, often worrying that she didn't keep her promise.

"Noted," he said, thoughts whirling around in his head.

"Let's get started. I want to get this over with."

CHAPTER 3

This guy got under her skin, no doubt about it. And she wasn't even totally sure why. From the moment she'd seen him, he'd irritated her in a different sort of way. All the inner peace knowledge she had went straight out the window, and she found herself wanting to simultaneously smack him across the face and kiss him.

But she was going to keep her composure no matter what. Now was not the time to let her hormones draw her closer to the wrong guy. He was here for one thing - to close the deal. To get what he wanted.

She hated to be so cynical. That was a side of herself she tried to push down when it popped up. It served no good purpose and only caused bad karma to come at her with the force of a freight train.

"So this is the best place to start, I guess," she said as they stood in the foyer. "Obviously, this is where guests enter. We have them sign their name in this book and then ring the bell."

"No one greeted me when I came in."

She gritted her teeth. "We don't exactly have the budget for front desk staff, Patrick."

"Right."

"Anyway, if you'll follow me. This is the powder room. Here's the storage closet where we keep extra yoga mats, blocks and so forth..."

"Blocks?"

"Have you never done yoga?"

He laughed as if it was a ridiculous question. "No."

She cocked her head and smiled slightly. "You should try it sometime. Might help you."

He squinted his eyes a bit, as if he wanted to prod further about what she meant, but he didn't. She was glad because right now she just wanted to finish up and go take something for the splitting headache she was getting.

"This hallway leads to our kitchen," she said as she opening the swinging door. "We buy pre-made meals mostly. I used to have a part-time chef, but that was the first cut I made when money became an issue."

He looked around the kitchen, occasionally touching the countertops or one of the appliances. "Not bad."

"Thanks for the ringing endorsement. I designed it myself."

"Oh."

Jill rolled her eyes as she turned and led them out of the kitchen. They went through another door onto the covered screened porch. It was almost as big as the bottom floor of the house all by itself.

"I opted for this big outdoor space rather than a formal living room inside. As you can see, we have the corner fireplace and these shutters can be locked tight over the screens to keep it warm during the cold winter months."

"I'm not much on the outdoors."

"Shocking," she said under her breath. "Have you ever even camped out?"

His face tightened inexplicably. "When I was a kid. I wasn't a fan."

"Oh. Well, I guess it all depends on who you're with."

"I guess," he said so softly that she almost didn't hear it.

"Ready to see the upstairs?"

"Sure."

He followed her upstairs as she gave the most bland tour she'd ever given. The last thing she wanted was for this guy to be excited about buying the place. On the other hand, if he did buy it, she wanted him to keep the building. It was her home. She'd literally breathed life into it herself. All those years of sketching the perfect home and business... and it could be gone in a few weeks.

When they'd finished the tour, they stood in the foyer again.

"It's getting a bit dark, so I guess you can show me the grounds tomorrow morning?"

"The grounds? Do you really need me for that, Patrick?"

"It would be preferable."

"Fine."

"Now, where is the closest hotel around here?"

Jill laughed out loud. "Hotel?"

"I need a place to stay for the night."

"Well, my dear, you're out of luck in these parts. We're the only game in town."

"Seriously?"

"Seriously."

"Then how can you be failing?"

She pursed her lips and sucked a sharp breath through her nose. "Excuse me?"

"If you're the only hotel..."

"This isn't a hotel! This is a retreat. A place that people come to de-stress, learn meditation, get away from life..."

"Oh, right. Well, maybe you should've tried the hotel idea?"

She rolled her eyes again. This guy was going to cause her eyes to get permanently stuck to the back of her skull.

"No one comes up here to stay, Patrick. They need an attraction. Something to draw them in."

"Like the resort and conference center I'm building?"

He had a point, but she sure wasn't telling him that. "Look, the closest place to stay is Mae's Motor Lodge down on the main road. It's about ten miles out behind the school bus graveyard. Rooms start at thirty for the night."

She turned and headed toward the stairs. "You've got to be kidding me. A motor lodge? What even is that? And a school bus graveyard?"

"Are you saying you're too good for that?"

"Yes, actually."

"Wow."

"How much for a room here tonight?"

"I don't rent rooms, Patrick."

"Five hundred?"

"My clients pay to stay here for a week or more. They get much more than a room..."

"Seven fifty?"

"I'm not a hotel..."

"One thousand?"

She was struggling now. That would pay her utilities this month. "Fine. Okay. But one night, and you're gone after our tour tomorrow?"

"I have no interest in being here any longer than I have to." He pulled out his wallet and counted out one thousand dollars. Jill was dumbfounded. How rich was this guy that he had so much money in his wallet? Maybe he was a white collar criminal or something.

"Good." She walked over to the table that had the log book on it, leafed through it and then pulled a key from the drawer. "Room three. It's down on the left, across from the bathroom."

"I don't have my own bathroom?"

"We share things here, Patrick."

"Good Lord."

He hesitantly took the key. "Dinner's at seven in the dining room. No dressy attire."

"All I have is dressy attire."

"Well, at least remove the jacket and tie. It makes everyone stressed to see those restrictive clothes."

"I feel like I'm in the Twilight Zone," he mumbled as he approached the stairs.

"Oh, and if you need a shower, better get in there before Ingrid. She's the lady with the red hair. She loves long showers, and you won't have a bit of hot water if she beats you to it."

He stared at her for a moment and then slowly walked up the stairs like he was heading to the electric chair.

Patrick stood in the middle of the room and looked around. It was as if the outdoors had seeped in through the windows with the log walls and rustic furniture. Why would anyone want this? What happened to high end linens and sleek, modern furnishings?

He dropped his leather bag, the one he'd bought in an Italian boutique, and sighed. This was going to be a long night. No way was he sleeping here longer than that.

He walked to the window, his expensive French dress shoes making a knocking noise on the solid oak floors. The land was much how he remembered it. Rolling hills mixed with towering blue tinged mountains. Darkness followed by light followed by more darkness. Much like his life.

He reached into his pants pocket and retrieved his cell phone. Pressing the buttons with more force than was needed, he called Jim at the bank.

"Jim here."

"Jim? It's Patrick." His voice was harsh and sharp.

"Uh oh. You don't sound happy. Not that you ever really do."

"Why have you sent me to this Godforsaken place?"

Jim chuckled. "Because you want that property, don't you?"

"Not bad enough to spend a night here. I feel like I'm standing in a tree house."

"Not a fan of the great outdoors?"

"No."

"Well, think about what a great deal you're going to get when we finally finish up the foreclosure on that place. It's a steal, man. Just tough it out, and you'll be happy you did."

"Doubtful."

"Have a good night," Jim said, amusement in his voice.

Patrick took in a deep breath. He was getting hungry, and there were no other viable options for dinner unless he wanted to snag himself a wild boar or something. And since he was fresh out of ammo, he was going to have to venture back downstairs soon.

Seeing her again had been harder than he imagined. She was still so beautiful, her eyes shining like pools of clear blue ocean. But they were pained. Stressed. Older. Wiser.

He hated this part of himself. The part where his heart

started to open and make him think - and possibly do - stupid things. Patrick didn't trust anyone, and that had served him well all these years. As much as he wanted to save her a second time, he wasn't going to do it. This was business, plain and simple.

"Knock knock," he heard her say from the other side of the door.

He opened it to find her standing there with two fresh towels folded in her arms. "Why didn't you actually knock instead of saying it?"

"Why do you overthink everything?" she retorted.

She handed him the towels and started to walk away, but she turned back and looked at him.

"What?"

"I feel like I've met you before."

Patrick froze in place under her gaze. The last thing he needed was for her to know who he was and then try to guilt him into saving her place. Not happening.

"Nope. We've never met."

She stared for a moment longer. "Weird. Well, anyway, dinner's in half an hour."

"What are we having?"

"Country fried steak, mashed potatoes with gravy and green beans. Oh, and peach cobbler for dessert."

"That doesn't sound very healthy."

"People come here for comfort, and I give it to them."

"Great. Sounds like a wonderful night for a heart attack," he said, shutting his door.

This guy was infuriating. And challenging. And sexy. And rich. And familiar.

Jill stood around the corner from his room and leaned against the log wall. What was it about him? Was it that she'd been alone for so long? Was it that she was always attracted to the wrong men? Or did she really know him from somewhere?

She wracked her brain. Had he been here before? Definitely not. Maybe she'd seen him in town? No, it wasn't that either. Yet, when she looked at his face, she felt a stirring. She knew him, and she didn't know why. And she felt drawn to him in a weird way, which was pretty disconcerting given that she wanted to smack him across the face for stealing her property out from under her.

"Hey there, Jill!" an older woman said as she left her room.

"Oh, hi, Alice. Have a nice nap?"

"Oh yes. I always sleep so great here."

"Me too. See you at dinner?"

"Of course! Can't wait for that cobbler!"

Jill walked down the stairs. The Retreat had started out as just a glimmer of a dream in her mind all those years ago. A place where people could recharge, hide from regular life for awhile and learn new skills to manage stress.

But what was she to do for her own stress?

She walked into the kitchen and started preparing plates for her few guests. Since Kaylee was gone, everything was on her now. She was the chef, the yoga teacher and the chief bottle washer. More stress. Great.

Thankfully - or not - this week was a slow one. Kids were going back to school, and parents weren't able to get away for a quick trip. So the only people staying with her right now were Ingrid, Alice and Winston.

These three people had been loyal to her over the years. Alice was in her seventies and had been a yoga teacher in her twenties. A lifelong vegan, she liked to come to The Retreat to get away from the stresses of life.

Ingrid was a fifty-something redhead with a fiery temper in her regular life, and that made for a lot of health issues including anxiety. She came to The Retreat once or twice a year to calm herself and reconnect.

And then there was Winston. He was in his eighties, and this area had been his home as a child. When he'd first come there, he was angry at the new development. But, over time, Winston had become like a grandfather to her. And he wanted to save The Retreat, but he didn't have a lot of money either. So he did what he could by paying to stay there a few times a year for a few days at a time, even though he was probably the least stressed person she knew.

She was thankful for these people who believed in her and The Retreat. It was their home away from home too, and she felt such a responsibility to save it. But how? She didn't have the money or resources to catch her payments up at this point. And it was clear the bank wanted to sell to Mr. Moneybags upstairs.

The guy seemed to be emotionless, so trying to tug at his heart strings wasn't going to work. She just felt trapped in an endless cycle of struggle. Much of her life had been this way. From being basically abandoned by her mother to working her butt off for years just to live her dream, nothing came easy for Jill.

For just one day, she wished things were easy. Simple. Peaceful.

"Need any help?" Ingrid asked from the doorway of the kitchen. Her hair was redder than the day before, obviously the result of a night of hair dye boxes littering the communal bathroom.

"No, but thanks. I've got it."

"You know, my guru taught me that it's okay to ask for help sometimes," she said with a sad smile.

"Your guru?"

"You, silly."

Jill laughed. "Oh, sweetie, I'm no guru." She turned and went back to stirring the sweet tea, the mound of wet sugar at the bottom of the pitcher feeling like concrete.

Ingrid walked over and hugged her from behind, her signature move. "It's okay not to be okay."

"You're like a walking motivational poster," Jill said with a chuckle.

"I'm worried about you, hon. You're so tense these days, and that just ain't like you."

Jill turned to her, struggling not to let the tears fall. One escaped anyway, like a wet little inmate running for freedom. "I'll be okay."

"Can I do anything at all, Jill? Anything?"

She thought for a moment and then handed her a pile of white plates. "You can set the table."

Ingrid grinned. "I'm on it, boss!"

Yes, Jill was so thankful for these amazing people. What was she going to do without them?

"Dinner's ready!" Jill called as she walked into the dining room with a huge bowl of mashed potatoes. Ingrid followed with the country fried steak and gravy bowl, which was ironic considering she was vegan. But Jill always made sure she had a nice big salad and a side of roasted potatoes to enjoy with everyone else.

Everyone was seated, except for Patrick, of course. He probably wasn't coming anyway.

"Sorry I'm late. I had a conference call that went over," he said as he walked into the room. He was still wearing his slacks and dress shoes, but he'd changed into a blue dress shirt, unbuttoned at the top, with the sleeves rolled up slightly. She assumed he was at least attempting to look more casual.

"No problem. Have a seat," Jill said, pointing to a chair across from where she'd be sitting. Winston eyed him closely, almost as if he knew who Patrick was.

"So, I see we have a newcomer. You been here before?" Winston asked, one of his bushy eyebrows raised.

Patrick cleared his throat. "No, sir. First time."

"You don't look like the type to come here."

Patrick cocked his head slightly. "There's a type?"

Jill tried not to laugh. It was nice to see Patrick uncomfortable for a bit, although it didn't make her the best host. Of course, she didn't invite him into her world in the first place.

"Where you from?"

"Atlanta."

"Figures," Winston said under his breath. Patrick looked at Jill for help, but she just smiled and scooped out a spoonful of mashed potatoes.

"How's the meditating going, Ingrid?"

"Oh, fine, I guess. I still can't clear my mind lately. I feel like I have that ADD thing."

Jill passed the dish of potatoes over to Patrick. He shook his head.

"You don't want potatoes?"

"Those are pretty high in carbs. I like to stay under..."

"Oh, good Lord, man, eat some potatoes!" Winston said, grumbling under his breath.

"Excuse me?"

34

"You young kids these days... worrying about carbs... just eat the food. Live a nice life. Stop worrying about all that ridiculousness."

Patrick smiled without making eye contact at Winston. Something about his smile gave Jill butterflies in her stomach. It looked good on him. Shame he didn't show it more often.

"Okay. I'll have a scoop," Patrick said, putting a small pile on his plate beside his steak.

Everyone started eating, but it was quieter than normal. Usually, there was boisterous conversation going on, and it helped distract Jill from her problems for awhile. But it was obvious everyone was wondering what Patrick was doing there.

"So, you all know that The Retreat is in trouble. I've been pretty honest about that. Mr. Scott is an investor. He's buying up a lot of the land around here to build a conference center and resort, and he wants this property..."

"I *need* this property."

"What?" Jill asked.

"I can't build my project without this piece. The logistics won't work." He stared down at his plate, jaw tightened.

"Oh. I wasn't aware you *had* to have my property," Jill said. She vaguely remembered the guy at the bank saying her property was in the middle of a proposed resort.

"Does it matter?" he asked, glancing at her.

"It does to me."

"You can't have this place," Alice said softly. "It's important to a lot of people."

"Look, I'm really sorry. I'm not the bad guy here. I'm just a business man trying to..."

"Make a buck," Winston said, his voice gruff as he pushed his chair back from the table and crossed his arms.

"That's what business people do, sir."

"Not all of them. I ran a successful business for forty years, Mr. Scott, and I never found the need to hurt others." The old man glared at Patrick.

"Why don't we just enjoy our dinner?" Jill said, trying to change the subject.

"The reality is that Jill is about to lose this place. It's going back to the bank. Wouldn't it be smarter if someone like myself bought it and rolled it into another project that would better this whole area?"

Winston's eyebrows furrowed together. "This area doesn't need to be better. It's perfect the way it is."

Patrick took a bite of his food, and the table went silent again. After everyone finished eating, the three other guests quietly excused themselves, leaving Jill alone with Patrick.

She watched him pull a pill bottle from his pocket and quickly slide one of the pills into his mouth, taking a sip of water.

"You okay?"

"Yeah. Why?"

"You're popping pills over there," she said, wiping her mouth with a napkin.

Patrick smiled slightly. "Getting old before my time. Stress will do that to you."

"Stress, huh? And what exactly does a billionaire have to be stressed about?"

His face fell slightly. "You know about that, huh?"

"Hard not to know that," she said, lying. In reality, she'd done a Google search on him before dinner to see who she was dealing with. After all, his wallet looked like an ATM machine, and she wasn't sure if he was some kind of con man. Nope, just a run-of-the-mill billionaire. It was very hard to bribe a man who had more money than everyone in the county put together.

"Well, stress affects everyone. I thought you would've known that."

She nodded. "You're right. Sorry. I wasn't trying to be judgmental."

He laughed. "I think you were, actually."

"Okay, maybe I was. But in fairness, you're not my favorite person at the moment."

His face changed again, almost as if she'd hurt him in some way. But he quickly regained his composure. "Sorry you feel that way, Jill. I guess I thought I was helping."

"Helping? You want to take my property, Patrick."

"But if the bank forecloses, it's gone anyway. I think you're taking your frustration out on the wrong person."

"What were those pills?" she asked, changing the subject.

"That's really none of your business."

"I know. But maybe there's a natural alternative to what you're taking. I was just going to give you a little friendly advice."

He smiled slightly. "Blood pressure pills. I was diagnosed about a year ago."

"You're mighty young to be suffering with that," she said. "Do you exercise?"

"I do weights occasionally. Otherwise, I don't have much time."

"You should try to do a hike while you're here. The mountain air will do you good. We have some great trails..."

"I'm leaving tomorrow after our tour, remember?"

"Right. Also, cut your salt intake down. I saw you load up your potatoes."

"Noted."

"Magnesium is really good for blood pressure too, so maybe get some of that."

"Will do."

"But the best thing I can recommend, short of reducing your stress levels, is to try meditation and some gentle yoga."

Patrick laughed. "Yeah, I'm not really the meditating type, in case you hadn't noticed."

"No one thinks they're the meditating type until they try it and see the benefits. Why don't you come to my morning class tomorrow? At least give it a try."

"I don't think so."

"Scared?"

"Um, no. I'm not scared of anything."

Jill smiled. "So you're not scared of anything? Then why don't you come to my class?"

"Because I don't have time."

"Seriously? That's the best you could come up with? It seems like you have all the time in the world because you can't take the tour until I finish class anyway."

She stood there with her hands on her hips, her signature move. Being short didn't allow for a lot of physical intimidation techniques, so this was all she had.

Patrick sighed. "Fine. If it will get you to stop talking right now and get me out of here faster tomorrow, I'll come to your silly class. But I'm telling you right now that I'm not going to become a yogi or a meditator."

"Great. I'll see you at seven," she said as he headed toward the stairs.

He stopped and turned back to her. "Hey, just out of curiosity... why didn't you tell the others that I'm a billionaire?"

She chuckled. "Why would I?"

"I don't know. A lot of people focus on that."

Jill leaned against the doorframe. "I guess that kind of thing just doesn't impress me."

Patrick smiled - a true genuine smile - and then walked upstairs.

CHAPTER 4

Patrick stood in his room, staring down at the plastic bag on his bed. He didn't know where she had managed to find him a pair of sweatpants and a T-shirt overnight, but somehow she did it. And now he really had no reason to avoid going to her class.

A part of him was enjoying their banter. He hadn't spent time with a woman like her in many years. Actually, he didn't even think he'd ever known a woman quite like her.

She seemed unimpressed by his financial status, which was refreshing. Most of the women he was around in the city only wanted him for one thing – his wallet.

He usually grew tired of these women rather quickly. Most of them were vapid, empty headed gold diggers, and he just wasn't into that. He liked women with more substance, but those were getting harder and harder to find the more money he made.

Patrick hadn't had a real relationship in several years. He did date one woman, Laura, for almost a year and actually considered proposing to her. He realized, just before he was about to buy the ring, that he was doing it more for status than for love. Last he heard, she was newly married and pregnant with her first child.

He wanted to be like all of his other successful friends and be married too. But as he looked around at their eventual failed and unhappy marriages, he decided he'd wait it out. He wanted the real thing, even if it meant he never found the right woman for him.

And, if he was honest with himself, he'd never quit thinking about Jill. Seeing her on the bridge that day fifteen years ago had touched something deep within his soul. And he had locked that feeling away as soon as he ran off into the woods. He never let anyone touch that space in his heart. He kept it walled off, almost protected. Patrick really don't know why given that it was only a brief encounter with a teenage girl on a bridge.

But it had meant something. He just didn't know what it meant.

And, of course, she had no idea when he ran away what he was actually running to. What was really going on in his life. She had no clue that he had been living his own personal hell when he ran into her that day.

He walked down the hallway and ran into Winston before he could make it to the staircase. The old man didn't like him at all, it seemed. Patrick found humor in that, but he also wished that he had somebody like Winston in his life. A grandfatherly figure. Somebody to talk about life issues with who didn't care how much money was in his bank account.

As much as he loved his business, he got tired of his life being a constant string of conversations about numbers and financials and return on investment.

Sometimes he wanted to sit down with an elder and talk about real stuff. But Patrick was guarded. He'd been through a lot in his life, and letting people in was extremely hard for him.

That was why it was so difficult to be around Jill. When he looked at her, at those eyes, all he wanted to do was let her in. He had this strong urge to sweep her up into his arms and never let her go again.

"Good morning, sir," Patrick said to Winston as they passed in the hallway. Winston stopped in his tracks, looking straight ahead.

"Morning," he said stoically. Patrick continued walking. "Hang on."

Patrick turned around and looked at the old man. He had the bushiest eyebrows he'd ever seen, almost like an unkempt Santa Claus without the beard. Winston walked a step closer, his face serious.

"I'm watching you. You need to know that."

"Excuse me?"

"Look, I was a Marine for more than twenty years. I may not look like much now, but I was pretty scrappy back in my day. And as far as I'm concerned, that little lady downstairs is like my granddaughter. I don't leave people I love behind, and I don't take too kindly to anyone trying to hurt them."

Patrick cocked his head to the side. "First of all, thank you for your service. I admire you for that, truly. Secondly, I'm not trying to hurt anyone, sir. I'm just doing business."

"This is all that Jill has. You realize that, right?"

"No, sir, I didn't realize that. But again, I'm really not here to make friends or enemies. I just want to see the property and make a good business decision. Surely you can understand that?"

The old man shook his head and grumbled. "No, but I'm

42

watching you. And if I see you hurting that girl in any way, I won't hesitate to..."

Patrick didn't let him finish. "I've got it. Thanks for the warning. Have yourself a good day," he said before turning and walking down the stairs. Old man or not, Marine or not, he wasn't going to stand there and be threatened by anybody.

As Patrick walked around the corner to the screened porch area, he saw her. She was wearing black yoga pants, no shoes and a tight fitting tank top. Her hair was swept up into a messy bun, tendrils of it hanging down next to her face. At the moment, she was alone in the room, waiting for her students to arrive, no doubt.

She turned and faced the mountains, her silhouette all that he could really see on the darkened porch. He leaned against the door frame and watched her as she reached her arms up to the sky, stretching tall.

Then she swept herself over, touching her feet. He watched her move like a sleek racehorse, strong and confident. She was tiny, but muscular.

Sensing he was there, she turned around, just a hint of a smile on her face.

"You actually showed up," she said matter-of-factly.

"Well, I kind of had to if I wanted to get the tour today. Plus you bought me these beautiful clothes, apparently." He felt like an idiot standing there in a gray T-shirt with puppies on it and a pair of black sweatpants.

"I thought puppies suited you," she said, stifling a laugh.

"Not much of a dog person."

"That doesn't surprise me."

"Not nice," he said, a quirk of a smile on his face.

This was certainly not the type of clothing he wore at home even when he was relaxing. Of course, relaxing wasn't something he did all that often. Normally he went straight from a business suit to his pair of prized silk pajamas.

"We can get started then." She waved him over into the middle of the room, a lone blue yoga mat on the floor.

"Wait a minute. I thought this was a class? Where are the other students?"

"This is more of a beginner class, and since my current guests are definitely not beginners, it's just going to be you and me."

"So we could've skipped this and gone straight to the tour," he said, slightly irritated.

"I like to keep to my schedule," she responded.

This was bad. Being alone with her for an extended period of time was not a good idea. But the way she was looking at him, expectation painted all over her face, didn't leave him room for argument.

"Okay... So what do I do?"

"Hang on. I'll be right back." She walked away, and he couldn't help but look at her backside in those yoga pants. It was something to behold. But he turned his attention back to the mountains off in the distance, not wanting the flushed red face of his Irish heritage to be the first thing she saw when she came back. It really was a beautiful view, no matter which way he turned his head, toward her or the mountains.

Moments later, he heard soft, relaxing music come across the outdoor speakers. It sounded like something you'd hear while getting a massage, a babbling brook mixed in with the sound of an acoustic guitar and an occasional wind chime.

She walked out in front of him and rolled out her own yoga mat about two feet away. She was facing him as she sat down, cross legged on the floor.

"Okay, you're going to want to cross your legs like mine. And then close your eyes, and keep your hands resting on your knees." Her voice was soft and soothing. He could see why classes with her were so attractive to students. She really should record some sort of sleep meditations and sell them on the Internet. Maybe he would suggest that to her.

He did as she said, without a word or argument. The faster he got through this, the faster he could be on his way. He just needed to see the property, so if he had to go through this whole charade of meditation first, that's what he would do. He was used to doing things he didn't want to.

"I want you to take in some deep, slow breaths. So breathe in, hold it for a count of four... That's good... And then slowly blow it out through your mouth for a count of seven... There you go... Very good."

At first, he found his mind wandering, thinking about everything from her yoga pants to the financials on another deal he was working on. But he breathed in and out over and over again, and he found that his mind was starting to clear. He felt calm. Almost peaceful. The feeling was foreign.

She had him breathe this way for several rounds. And then she instructed him to clear his mind as much as possible and just continue breathing naturally. She told him every time his mind wandered, he needed to have a mantra in his head. She suggested simply trying the word "peace".

Every time he thought of something, he redirected his mind to the word peace. A few minutes later, it was over. Or at least it seemed like a few minutes.

When he opened his eyes, she was smiling, her eyes wide.

"What?"

"Do you realize you just meditated for twenty minutes straight? I don't think I've ever seen a beginner do that!"

Patrick was surprised. It seemed like only a few minutes. And he felt so relaxed, almost like he'd had a few too many cocktails.

"I guess I had a good teacher."

"How do you feel?"

"Very relaxed," he said, an easy smile on his face. He couldn't believe it really. Doctors had given him anti-anxiety medication before, and he didn't recall feeling this good even after taking one of those. Maybe she was onto something. But he would never tell her that.

"Good. Now, before we go out on our tour, let's do a little bit of yoga to stretch out." She stood up on her mat and waited for him to stand. Honestly, he felt like he wanted to take a nap but decided to play along with her just to avoid an argument that might spoil his calm mood.

"Okay, the first thing I'm going to show you is downward facing dog pose."

"Dog pose?"

"Don't let the name throw you. This is really good for your back as well as the back of your legs. First, we'll start by warming up with a forward bend, and then downward dog. So what I need you to do is bend from your waist..." As she showed him the correct position, she ran her hand down his back, walking around his body and touching him in different places to make sure he was doing the position correctly.

Shivers ran up and down his body over and over, like an electric current that he couldn't turn off. No matter how many dates he'd been on in his life, he'd never felt anything like this. Electricity was the only way to describe it.

She taught him several poses, pushing and stretching his

body in ways he never imagined. Suddenly he realized he hadn't thought about taking the tour for quite a while. All he wanted to do was continue stretching with her, letting her run her hands all along his back and legs and arms.

Maybe he really did need to talk to a dating service or one of those matchmakers his friends were always talking about. Or maybe he just needed to get a massage. But something about the way Jill ran her hands along his skin made him feel comfortable. Safe. Alive. But most of all, it made him feel peaceful for the first time he could ever really remember in his life.

Jill had to admit that she enjoyed the meditation and yoga class she had given Patrick. And, much to her surprise, he had done very well.

She didn't think she had ever seen someone meditate for so long on the first try. And he really seemed to enjoy it, which was surprising.

But now, as she put on some warmer clothes, the realization that she had to take him for the tour as promised was finally hitting her. And the last thing she wanted to do was show him around her property and wait for him to snatch it out from under her.

He was a freaking billionaire. She wasn't really impressed by his wealth because money wasn't her main goal in life. But she was well aware of all the things he could do with that much money, including taking her property.

When she was logical about it, she knew that he wasn't actually stealing her property. He was simply buying something that she was already losing. That wasn't his fault, but he was a great person to take it out on.

She put on a thick brown sweater, her favorite pair of skinny jeans and some knee-high boots. When she walked downstairs, Patrick was already standing in the foyer waiting for her.

And he looked pretty dang good. Surprisingly, he had on a sweater and some jeans himself. She wondered why he didn't wear those to dinner the last night.

"You're looking mighty casual today," she said with a smile. "Where have you been hiding those clothes?"

"Actually, I slipped out this morning after our class and went down to the only store I could find within twenty miles of here. Not the nicest clothes but I couldn't believe how low the prices were." He looked down at his sweater with a certain kind of pride on his face.

"Those are what we call 'regular people prices', Patrick," Jill joked.

"Very funny. So, I'm feeling pretty relaxed after our class this morning. I'm all rejuvenated and ready to see the property."

She couldn't help it, but her face fell. The property. Her baby. The thing she loved most on this planet.

"Right. Well, I guess we should get going. We'll start with the grounds closest to the house and move our way outward."

He followed her out the door, and they walked around the main grounds near the building. She showed him the outbuilding where they kept the yard equipment, and then showed him some of her very favorite views from the main property. They made their way down the trails to other parts of the property, most of it wooded with very few open spaces. He made notes on his phone and talked about plans for certain areas if he were to get the land. Jill tried to ignore it, tried not to think about the fact that she really wanted to push him off the nearest cliff to keep him from signing papers to buy her place.

But she also didn't want to live in the state prison.

"So, do you want to take a little break?" she asked him as they meandered around.

"Sure. I am a little worn out. This is a pretty big piece of land."

They sat down on some big rocks overlooking the Blue Ridge Mountains. It was one of her favorite places on the whole property. Well, maybe her second favorite place. She hadn't shown him the first favorite.

"You know, when I first bought this place, the real estate agent brought me here and showed me this view. I was immediately hooked."

"I can see why."

"I remember sitting here the day after I closed with a notebook. I was making all kinds of plans, you know, for the future. What this place would be like in five years, ten years. I never thought about what would happen if I totally failed."

"I'm really sorry, Jill. I wish it had worked out for you."

She had a feeling that he was actually being sincere. "It's my own fault. When I look back, I was so excited about the business and helping people that I didn't pay enough attention to my finances. I made an improvement, a specific one, on this property that used up a lot of my funds. I mismanaged my money, plain and simple."

He bumped his shoulder against hers. "Don't beat yourself up too bad. This was your first business, and everybody makes mistakes when they first start out."

"Even you?"

"Even me. The very first business I tried to start failed miserably. But if I hadn't tried, I never would've changed course and ended up where I am today."

"And where is that exactly?"

"What do you mean?"

"I mean, yes, you have a lot of money and a great business, it sounds like. But what about your personal life, Patrick? Anyone special?" She didn't know why she was asking. She didn't really want to know. Okay, she did want to know. But she didn't *want to* want to know.

He smiled slightly. "Nobody special right now."

"I get the feeling that you're kind of locked down. As if you don't like to talk about your personal life very much. Or maybe a personal life isn't even important to you?"

"And I get the feeling that you like to talk about feelings a lot."

Jill giggled. "It's my business. My job is to open people up to every part of themselves."

"Oh yeah? And you think I'm not open to myself?"

"Look, all I know is that if I had one week with you here participating in everything I offer, you'd be a different man when you left."

"That sounds a lot like a dare." He raised an eyebrow as he looked at her.

"Okay, so maybe it is a dare. I'm sure that you wouldn't take this particular dare because it would require you to stay here for a whole week, and I don't think that Patrick Scott is up for that kind of a challenge."

He looked at her carefully, his eyebrow still raised. She could tell he was mulling it over, obviously not a man who liked to shrink from challenges. But then he changed the subject.

"You mentioned there was another part of this property that you feel like you spent too much money improving. Can you show me that?"

She knew she had to. He wasn't going to let it go. But the

last thing she wanted to show Patrick right now was the most special place on earth to her. That was a place she liked to keep reserved for just herself, but now she was going to have to share it with someone else. And the only person she ever wanted to share that place with disappeared into the woods fifteen years ago.

CHAPTER 5

Patrick had to admit that he was enjoying walking the property with Jill. A part of him looked at her as if she was someone he had just met, but then there was the other part of him that knew the secret. She didn't seem to recognize him at all, and he wanted to keep it that way. Business was hard enough without putting emotions into it. And if she found out that he was the boy who stopped her from jumping all those years ago and then kissed her before running off into the woods, she would certainly have expectations that he would save her property like he'd saved her that day.

He couldn't blame her. It was probably the right thing to do. But he had learned long ago that mixing emotion and business was a bad idea. So he preferred to keep it this way. Do things as simply and easily as possible without upsetting the apple cart.

But he had to admit that when he looked at her, growing more and more upset about potentially losing her property, he wanted to ride in on a white horse and save her. Somewhere deep down, that was still the man he was. He wanted to keep people from hurting, from experiencing pain. But time and circumstances had toughened him up and put some kind of thick callus around his heart.

And all of that had worked really well for him until he walked in to The Retreat and saw Jill.

"Okay, the place I want to show you is right up here over the hill."

He followed her up a steep incline, which was covered in newly fallen leaves as Fall was approaching. It was beautiful this time of year, and it would only get better as the weeks wore on. He remembered from his childhood that the leaves would turn yellow and then a vibrant orange before finally falling to the ground in an inevitable circle of life moment.

As they came over the crest of the hill, both of them panting from the steepness of the incline, Patrick's mouth fell open. Luckily she was in front of him and didn't see his initial reaction.

The bridge. The place they met. The one place in the world he wanted to see again but at the same time never wanted to see again. He knew it was somewhere close by, but he had no idea it was on her property. Now it all made sense. Why she chose this place. Why she was having such a problem leaving it.

In an instant, he was taken back to that moment as a fifteen-year-old boy when he walked over the hill and saw a beautiful young girl standing there. As he'd gotten closer, he'd noticed her eyes. They were a steely blue color, like nothing he'd ever seen.

Before he knew it, all thoughts about his own pressing problems left his mind. His sole focus had been on saving her. He was never the same when he walked off the bridge that day.

She turned around and looked at him. "This bridge was

in shambles when I visited here as a kid. It means a lot to me, for reasons I won't go into. In fact, it means more to me than all of this land combined. The whole reason I bought this property was to save this bridge because this bridge saved me."

He felt emotion welling up inside of him. He hadn't cried in so many years he couldn't even remember the last time. But for a moment, he felt like he might. In true Patrick fashion, he pulled himself together quickly.

"So, this is what you sank your money into?"

She smiled sadly. "Seems stupid, I know. But I didn't want this bridge to fall into that ravine and be forgotten. I could never forget this place. "

"It's not stupid. Saving something that you believe in, something that means a lot to you, is never stupid."

She smiled slightly and cocked her head. "Really? I'm surprised to hear you say something like that. You don't strike me as the sentimental type, no offense."

"None taken. But I totally get why you did this. And you did an amazing job having it restored. I really like that you kept the red paint.“

She looked confused for a moment. "How would you know that? You've never been here before."

"Oh... I just mean... I assume it was pretty bad from your description...And most covered bridges are painted red..." he said, stumbling over his words.

"Yes, it was a mess. I spent a lot of money and hired contractors who understood the historical accuracy that I needed to bring it back to life." She stared at the bridge, a faraway look in her eyes. Of course, Patrick knew why she had that look on her face. She wasn't looking at the bridge at all. She was looking into the past.

"So did you have any plans for this place?"

"You'll think it's stupid."

"No I won't. Tell me."

She smiled broadly. "Well, for one thing, I had high hopes of having my own wedding here someday. Walking down the middle of the bridge from one side to the other... I guess a girl can dream."

"A wedding, huh? And that's it?"

She lightly punched him on the arm. "For a woman, a wedding is a pretty big deal. But, I also had it restored because I thought I could rent it out for people who wanted to have weddings here too. Make it a whole venue. I was going to build a gazebo on the other side where the guests would sit. I just never got the chance. Once I opened up The Retreat, things started to fall apart after a couple of years and I just didn't have the money to do the marketing needed to get people to come here."

Patrick felt terrible for her. He knew what failure felt like, and Jill was definitely beating herself up. In her eyes, she'd failed at her business and at saving the bridge.

"So, do you want to go take a look?" she asked, a hopeful tone in her voice.

Patrick froze in place for a moment. Did he really want to go back up there? Would he be able to keep himself from wanting to grab her and finish that kiss that was started fifteen years ago? Again, he pulled himself together.

"Sure."

They walked up the rest of the hill and onto the edge of the bridge. The familiar wooden slats were still there, but restored. As they walked along, he looked at all of the little details that she had made sure were done.

As they made their way down, they stopped right in the

spot where she was standing that day. He knew it was no accident. There were tall railings in the spot where she was going to jump that day, surely a preventative measure to make certain no one ever thought of that idea again.

"This is amazing. The views are really stunning. You did a great job restoring this, Jill."

She took in a deep breath and slowly blew it out. "This place is why I'm so upset, Patrick. I could build The Retreat somewhere else. My customers would follow me. But I could never get this place back. It just... It means a lot to me."

He wanted to ask her what it meant. Why she was so attached to it. Even though he already knew the answer, he kind of wanted to see if she mentioned him. But the thought of doing that and risking her realizing who he was stopped him from opening his mouth.

"You have my word that if I buy this place, I won't tear down the bridge." He hadn't meant to say it, but it just flew out of his mouth. In reality, it was in a terrible place as far as the layout of the conference center and resort. Tearing it down would be a lot more cost-effective, but this was where being a billionaire had its perks. He could do whatever he wanted.

She grinned broadly. "Oh, thank you, Patrick! That really means a lot. Maybe one day I can come back and visit or something." She hugged his neck tightly without warning, and Patrick stood there frozen, unable to believe he was touching her again... on the bridge, of all places. Every emotion he'd felt that day came rushing back. Feelings long since pushed to the deepest parts of his soul bubbled up and threatened to make him do things he'd regret.

And then she stepped back, her face slightly flush from embarrassment. "I'm so sorry about that. It's just that the bridge is most important. Even though I'll lose my business, my income, the friends I've made here... well, at least the bridge will continuing living on."

Something about the way she seemed to have already resigned herself to losing the property made him sad. Sadder than he expected. Normally when someone said something like that, it indicated he was going to get the deal he wanted. For a moment, he felt like he didn't want this deal at all.

But if he didn't buy it, who would? And what would they do to the bridge? He couldn't take that chance.

As they stood there quietly staring out over the Blue Ridge Mountains, Patrick felt conflicted. Should he buy this place out from under her? Should he throw away his chances at the conference center and resort that he had agreed to with his partners? Should he open himself up to all kinds of legal trouble in the process?

He reached into his pocket and pulled out one of his blood pressure pills. Popping it in his mouth, he swallowed hard, trying to do it without being noticed by Jill.

Her head swung around and she looked at him. "Are you popping blood pressure pills again?"

"I just realized I forgot to take it this morning because I was so super relaxed after our meditation."

"Patrick, I know we don't know each other very well, but I really do care about your health. Remember that dare?" she asked with a grin on her face.

"Yes..."

"One week. Give me one week to prove to you that this place can change lives."

He sighed and shook his head. "It won't mean anything, Jill. I still have to buy this place."

"Maybe so, but at least let me prove to myself, one final

time, that I have what it takes to change lives. It might be my last chance to do that here, Patrick. If I can help you, it will give me the confidence I need to start over."

Before he could stop himself yet again, Patrick nodded his head and agreed. He would give her one week to prove to herself that she could really help people. Maybe that was the last gift he could give to her before they parted ways again.

She couldn't believe he agreed to it. Secretly, she hoped that him staying at The Retreat for a week would get him to understand the importance of the work that she did. Maybe he would talk to the bank and get them to stop the foreclosure. Maybe he would loan her the money to save her place. In fact, she'd dreamed up a host of fairytale ways he could rescue her, none of which were probable.

She tried not to think about the fact that he needed her property to buy the rest of the land that he required for his conference center and resort.

Jill knew she wasn't thinking clearly right now. She was grasping at straws, trying anything to potentially save her business. And not just her business, but her life. This place had saved her life all those years ago, and she felt like history was on repeat.

This time, of course, she had no intentions of standing on the edge of the bridge. But she did feel like everything she knew and loved was about to be ripped out from under her and there wasn't a thing in the world she could do about it.

"Hey there, Jill," Winston said as he walked up behind her.

"Oh, hey, Winston. How are you doing today?"

"Well, I'm a little concerned, to be honest."

"Concerned? Is something wrong with your room?"

"No, honey. I am concerned about you."

Jill walked over and sat down at the kitchen table, patting the area across from her for Winston to join her.

"Why are you concerned about me?"

"I know that you are just torn to pieces about losing this place. I'm a little worried that this new guy is going to break your heart."

She cocked her head to the side. "Break my heart? We are certainly not interested in each other like that, Winston," she said with a smile.

"Sweetie, I didn't just fall off the turnip truck. I know what it looks like when two people are attracted to each other."

Jill's face flushed. "I think you're misreading the situation. He's only here to learn more about this place so that he can roll it into his real estate deal. Trust me, I'm under no assumption that he's interested in me at all."

"I think you're wrong about that. I've been watching the boy's face every time he looks at you. Might make me seem like a stalker, but you're like my granddaughter so I feel a need to watch after you."

Jill smiled. "I appreciate you looking out for me. I really do. You know I don't have any family, except a sister who doesn't even talk to me and a mother who forgot I exist, apparently. But I think you're overreacting on this one."

He reached across the table and touched her hand. "Just be careful. Sometimes matters of the heart can cloud our judgment pretty bad."

"Well, there's no reason to worry. I promise. I know exactly where I stand with Patrick Scott."

~

"So you want me to go hiking?" Patrick asked, his eyes popping open like someone had just jumped out and scared him.

"Yes, hiking. It's what we do up in this area. I don't see what the big deal is. We walked a lot the other day."

Patrick laughed. "That was different. This is actual hiking. I'm not really sure what the difference is, but it seems more dangerous."

Jill giggled "Come on, Patrick. You promised to trust me and we're only on the first day. I wouldn't do anything that would put us in harm's way."

"I know there are bears in these woods. And probably bobcats. Why in the world do we need to go out there for you to prove that you can help people?"

She really hadn't expected him to give her so much problem about going hiking which only made her want to drag him out there all the more.

"Look, you'll have a great time. We'll be back before dinner. And I think it will help you to clear your mind and lower your blood pressure, which is what I'm trying to do."

He stood there for a moment, obviously pondering the options in his head. "Fine. But I don't have any hiking boots."

"Don't worry, I'm way ahead of you there." She reached behind the table and pulled out a bag with a pair of brand new hiking boots.

"How did you know my size?"

"I might have snuck into your room and looked at your dress shoes. I hope these fit."

"Jill, you shouldn't be buying things for me. Given your situation..."

She clenched her jaw. "I'm not destitute, Patrick. I know I might seem to be that way since you're a freaking billionaire, but I can afford a pair of cheap hiking boots."

He smiled. "You really don't care about how much money I have, do you?" He seemed to be pleased by that.

"No, I really don't. Money isn't what impresses me about a person."

"So what does impress you?"

Jill stepped forward, still holding the bag out to him. "I'll tell you what. I'll answer any questions you have as soon as we're out on the hiking trail."

Patrick sighed and took the bag from her hand.

She was a tough nut to crack. From the outside, with her petite stature and job that involved yoga and meditation, someone could have incorrectly assumed that Jill was a pushover. He was finding out that she definitely wasn't.

As he laced up his hiking boots, he watched her talking to the other guests as they went on about their day. Alice was planning to go birdwatching. Ingrid was going into the woods to do some quiet meditation. And Winston... Well, he seemed to just be watching Patrick.

Patrick had the distinct impression that Winston didn't like him. And that he didn't want Patrick to be around Jill. But unfortunately, she was the owner of the place and he didn't have much choice. Plus, he had ridiculously agreed to this one week stay at The Retreat.

Just as they were about to walk out the door, Patrick's phone rang in his pocket.

"Sorry, I need to take this. It's my assistant. I'll be just a minute," he said. Jill walked outside and waited for him. "Hello?"

"Hey, boss, where are you? I thought you were coming back today."

"Oh, yeah, I forgot to give you a call this morning. Listen, I've decided to stay up here for another week."

"You're kidding, right? You're not exactly the outdoorsy type." Patrick paused for a moment. People really didn't know what he'd been through as a kid.

"Well, I'm trying something new. So just stay in touch with me on my cell phone, and I'll be checking text and email. I have a couple files on my desk that might need some follow up."

"Okay. Good luck. Don't get eaten by a bear."

Patrick definitely didn't think that was funny.

He walked outside, slipping his phone back in his pocket.

"Hand it over," Jill said.

"What?"

"Your cell phone. You can't take that out on the hiking trail with you."

"You have to be kidding me. Why do I need to leave my cell phone here? I'll just turn it on silent."

Jill held out her hand "Nope. No cell phones while we are out in nature. It takes away from the experience. Plus you have the electromagnetic field around your phone..."

Patrick held up his hand. "Fine. Please do not explain what the electromagnetic field has to do with anything. I'll just trust your judgment on this one." He chuckled and handed her the phone.

Jill leaned back inside the door. "Winston, can you put this in the cell phone box please?"

Patrick cocked his head to the side. "Hey, why did you give my phone to Winston?"

"Don't worry. He can barely use his own cell phone. He's just going to lock it in the box that we keep other cell phones in that somehow make their way up to The Retreat."

"This is the weirdest place I've ever been," Patrick said as he started to follow her up the trail.

CHAPTER 6

As they walked along, Jill wondered what she had gotten herself into. He had barely spoken two words, and they been walking for almost ten minutes now. Maybe he wasn't happy that he had roped himself into this one week stay. And in all reality, she wasn't sure why he even agreed to it.

"Are you okay?" she finally asked.

He chuckled. "Well, Jill, I'm more accustomed to sitting in an office in a very expensive ergonomic chair for most of the day. This is a little above my pay grade."

She laughed and looked at him. "Not to inflate your ego too much, but you look pretty physically fit. I'm surprised that this would be difficult for you."

"We're in the mountains. This isn't exactly the typical terrain I see in my gym when I'm on the treadmill."

"Maybe you should increase your incline next time. You really want to challenge your heart. Especially with your blood pressure problems."

He stopped for a moment to catch his breath. They hadn't even gotten to the most difficult part of the hike yet, so she was a little concerned about his stamina.

"You're very concerned about my blood pressure, aren't you?"

"I am."

"What I don't understand is why? I mean, you don't know me. We probably won't ever see each other again after this week."

For some reason, that statement made her a little sad. She was used to building friendships with people and really placed a high value on relationships. She hadn't had many good relationships in her life, including with her own family, so building a family that wasn't related to her by blood had always been really important. And the well-being of the people in her circle of friends was a top priority.

"Because I really care about people, Patrick. Is that so hard for you to understand?" They walked over and sat down on an outcropping of rocks overlooking a small valley.

"I guess it is. Most of my life is filled with numbers and file folders and looking at properties. I don't have a whole lot of time to think about other peoples' health issues."

She pulled a bottle of water out of her backpack and handed it to him. "We are all a part of humanity. I think sometimes people who work in office buildings and don't get out in nature or to socialize with other people, well, it makes them a little bit detached."

"I get around people. I go to dinner parties and business meetings and..."

"But do you do anything that doesn't have a purpose that ends with the almighty dollar?"

He pondered for a moment and then shook his head. "No."

"You say that like it's no big deal. Don't you understand that life isn't just about money?"

"I get that it's that way for some people. But for me, my

life revolves around money. It's the one thing I can control. It's constant. I know how to make it on demand, and that makes me feel comfortable."

"I would beg to disagree. That makes you have high blood pressure."

He chuckled. "Touché. But at least I can afford the best doctors."

She rolled her eyes. "So, tell me what it's like to be a billionaire. I mean, where does your stress come from?"

Patrick looked at her, his eyebrows knitted together in confusion. "Really? Where does my stress come from?"

"Yeah. I mean, most of the stress I have in my life is money related, so I assume that being a billionaire would be less stressful in the financial department."

He shook his head and laughed. "Not really. We all have the same fears deep down. Losing everything. Messing up. Becoming a great big failure. Billionaire or not, I think that's pretty universal. And failing as a billionaire would be a pretty huge amount of failure for one person."

"Surprising. I guess I thought that having a lot of money would take that stress away."

Patrick looked out over the ridge. "Sometimes, I think stress comes from things that happened in the past. And they just color every part of your life for the rest of your life."

"Wow, that's kind of a pessimistic way to look at life. You don't think you can overcome things that happened in childhood? "

"Well, if you can, I haven't figured out the secret to that."

"I guess I have this innate sense that everything is going to be all right even when it seems like it's not. I don't know where that comes from."

"That's good to hear. I know things will work out for you, Jill. You've been in worse situations than this."

As soon as he said it, his face fell. It almost looked like all of the blood drained out of his body. What did he mean by that? She hadn't told him anything about her upbringing, so how could he know she'd been through anything worse?

"What are you talking about? What worse things have I been through?" She studied him carefully.

"I... I just meant that everyone has been through worse things. I mean I would imagine. I know I have."

He stammered and stuttered over his words, and this wasn't the first time he'd done that. Jill had the distinct impression that he was keeping something from her, but she had no idea what it was. Maybe he had researched her past? But it wasn't like her family problems were common knowledge on Google.

"So what kinds of things have you been through, Patrick?" she asked, hoping to get some insight on why this guy's stress level was so high.

"I don't like to talk about it."

"I understand, but sometimes if you open up..."

"Jill, please. Look, I know you're trying to help and all of that. And I'm willing to give you a chance to help me learn new stress reduction techniques, but my private life is not open for discussion. I'm here on business, not to pour out all of my personal thoughts and history."

She sucked in a sharp breath and blew it out slowly. This guy was tough. And he was definitely hiding something, probably several things. It made her uncomfortable, but it made her feel sorry for him at the same time.

"You're right. I'm sorry. I'm just used to people telling me things. It's really hard for me to help you figure out what's causing so much stress if I don't know anything about you. Maybe you could just share some basic things about yourself?"

He loosened up a little bit and smiled ever so slightly. "Fine. I am about to turn thirty-one years old. I run a commercial real estate company that's very successful. I live in a penthouse apartment overlooking Atlanta. I have three cars including a sweet little red Ferrari. Oh, and my favorite color is blue."

Jill sighed. "Do you realize that you didn't tell me anything about yourself?"

"What? I just told you several things about myself."

"No, you basically rattled off your resume other than telling me your favorite color. I don't care about your business or your penthouse or your cars. I'm trying to find out who you are, as a person."

He groaned and ran his fingers through his hair. "I don't know what you want from me."

"Okay, let's try something different. Let me ask you some general questions, nothing overly personal. Does that work?"

"I guess."

"Okay, when you wake up in the morning, what's the first thing you think about?"

He thought for a moment. "Well, I think about my schedule and where I need to be first. I think about the meetings I have that day, deals I'm closing, problems I need to solve."

"Got it. And when you go to bed at night, what is usually the last thing you think about?"

"Pretty much the same stuff. I usually make a list of all the things I need to do the next day and then pop a sleeping pill."

"What's your favorite thing to do on the weekend?"

He laughed. "These are the most random questions."

"Just answer the question."

"Well, I usually end up working in my office, or sometimes my home office, on the weekends."

"But don't you have any hobbies? Friends you hang out with? Places you go to unwind on the weekend?"

"Not really. Running the kind of business I do doesn't allow for a lot of free time. I might occasionally get a glass of wine with a client or do a little shopping for a new suit."

Jill laughed. "I think I know your problem, Patrick."

"Oh yeah? And what is that?"

"You don't have anything that relaxes you. You don't have a girlfriend or a wife or someone you love that can feed into your life. You don't have hobbies or friends that you can just hang out with and be yourself. You're always 'on'. You're always the face of your company and constantly thinking about money and deals and problems and properties. You're one dimensional."

"Wow. Thanks a lot. One dimensional."

She touched his arm. "I don't mean that as a put down. I mean that you don't have any thing else to look forward to. You're not feeding the other parts of yourself. When you have so much money, every deal is just a job. You don't need more money, you need more love. More time. More smiles."

"And how are you suggesting that I get those things?"

"Well, for one thing, this week I suggest that you completely unplug. No contact with the outside world, but most especially your business. Put somebody else in charge while you're here. It's basically like putting yourself in the shop, much like you would one of your prized cars. Completely focus on yourself and let everyone else do the worrying for you."

"I can't do that," he said immediately.

"Patrick, the reason you built this huge company and made it so successful was so that you could have freedom.

Financial freedom, yes. But what about time freedom? Why have you hired all of these people if you're not going to let them work and take the load off of you?"

He sat there for a moment, obviously contemplating what she was suggesting. "I see what you're saying, but now is a really bad time for me to just go completely silent."

"It's never going to be a good time. And it certainly won't be a good time if you drop dead of a heart attack from all the stress."

He laughed. "Boy, you know how to drive your point home. Okay, fine. I will call my assistant when I get back and let him know that I will check in at the end of the week but otherwise I am out of commission for the next seven days."

Jill smiled broadly. "Great! That will give us time to totally focus on helping you make some changes that will reduce your stress and improve your health."

They stood and started walking up the trail again. "I still don't know why you want to help me. After all, I'm the man that you think is stealing your business from you."

She stopped and looked around before looking back at him. "I don't know. I guess in my heart, I want to help people. A long time ago, somebody helped me when I was in a really bad situation. I've spent the rest of my life trying to pay it forward since I can never say thank you to that person."

Patrick shifted uncomfortably, looking down at his feet. "Why can't you say thank you?"

"Because I don't know where he is. I don't even know his last name. But all those years ago, a stranger saved my life and that made my purpose to save other peoples' lives."

Patrick sat on one of the decks overlooking the mountains. This place really was serene and peaceful. And those were two words that he didn't use lightly.

A part of him was glad that he agreed to this dare. Detaching from work for a few days was something that was long overdue, but that didn't mean it wasn't difficult.

As long as he could remember, Patrick liked to control things. So much of his childhood had been out of his control that he'd spent most of his adulthood trying to keep all the balls in the air by himself. No matter how many people he hired, he never put one hundred percent trust in anyone.

Trusting someone was dangerous.

As he sat there, drinking very strong coffee that Jill had made after their hike, he looked around at the property. Soon, it would likely be rolled into the conference center and resort he would build. The trees would be knocked down. The land would be cleared. The views would change.

A part of him was actually sad when he thought about it, but then his business mind reminded him how much money he would make for himself and others. How many jobs he could provide in the local area. And how progress had to happen. Things couldn't always just stay the same. Progress always demanded change.

"Oh, sorry. I didn't know you were out here," Jill said as she walked through the sliding door leading out onto the deck.

"No, it's fine. Please come and join me."

He pointed to the other rocking chair. This particular deck was off of the upstairs loft area. It provided one of the better views of the property.

"So what are you doing out here?"

"I am doing what I was instructed to do. Clearing my mind of all things business."

She chuckled. "Good. Then I should go back inside so I don't interrupt you."

As she started to stand up, Patrick's stomach growled so loudly that he was sure it probably scared the local wildlife. Jill looked at him and smiled.

"You don't happen to be hungry, do you?"

"Honestly? I'm starving. I don't think my body is quite used to burning so many calories in a day."

Standing in front of him, she reached out her hand. "Come on. It's time for me to start cooking dinner, and I could use an extra set of hands."

He stared at her hand for a moment. They looked much the same as they did fifteen years ago. He didn't know how he even remembered what they looked like. So many brief glimpses from that day were seared in his brain forever. He reached up and took her hand, standing in front of her.

"I'm not much of a cook, I should probably admit that now."

She let go of his hand, and he felt an immediate void that he wasn't expecting. "I wasn't a very good cook when I came here either. But you learn to improvise. I might be able to show you a trick or two. Although I'm sure that you have a personal chef back in the city, if armageddon ever happens and you have to make yourself some eggs, I can show you how."

Patrick laughed. He was laughing a lot more in the last couple of days than he probably had all year. Something about this place, this woman, had brought him here yet again. The mountains had called him, and he had answered. And everything felt pretty scary right about now.

CHAPTER 7

Jill pulled her hair up into a messy bun and then sat down to put on her sneakers. Every morning was an early morning for her. Running The Retreat by herself now was proving to be more difficult than she thought. Even losing her part-time assistant had made things so much more hectic and exhausting.

Although she never wanted to lose her business, a part of her was looking forward to a time when she didn't have to be so stressed out. Who knew that helping other people with their stress could be so stressful?

Last night had been fun. Patrick had come to the kitchen with her, and they had worked on making some pies for the week. Then they made a very simple dinner for everyone of turkey sandwiches and chips. Again, Winston had sat at the table with a worried and irritated look on his face. He definitely didn't like Patrick for some reason.

"Early start?" Patrick said as he came down the stairs, already completely dressed.

"I get an early start every day."

"Going somewhere? "

"I actually have to go into town for some supplies. We're running low on some things in the pantry."

"Need some help?"

"No, it's okay. I know you do your meditation in the morning, and I wouldn't want to interfere with that."

"Actually, I already did my meditation this morning in my room," he said, proudly jutting out his chin. "So, why don't we take my car into town, and I can help you pick up some things?"

Jill smiled. "Actually, I have to get quite a lot and I don't think your little car is going to do the trick. But we can take my truck," she said. The look on his face was priceless.

"I've never driven a truck before," he said.

"Patrick, nobody asked you to drive," she said as she smacked him on the shoulder and walked to the front door.

They walked outside and over to Jill's beat up red truck. It sat up high and required her to climb to get inside, but she loved it. Something about an old pick up truck riding along the mountain roads made her feel at home.

"Nice truck."

She giggled. "It might not be much, but it's mine. And nobody can take it away from me." She knew she shouldn't have said the last part. Making him feel guilty for something he wasn't really doing wrong was probably getting kind of old. And she was supposed to be helping him, not trying to make him feel bad.

"Shall we go?" he asked without cracking a smile.

They walked over to the truck, and surprisingly he walked around and opened the door for her.

"Thank you."

After he shut the door, he walked around his side and jumped up into the seat next to her. She had to admit he looked pretty at home sitting there. For a split second, she

74

couldn't imagine him driving that fancy car that was parked a few feet away.

"So where are we going?"

"Well, I need to get some groceries but I also wanted to get a few things that we need around the property. Some new pavers for the sidewalk near the garden. Some extra fencing for the garden to keep the deer out..."

She pulled down the driveway and out onto the main road, which was orange dirt.

"Jill, if you don't mind me asking... Why are you buying things to improve the property if you're going to lose it?"

Hearing him say that she was going to lose the property had bothered her before, but she was starting to make her peace with it. She didn't like it, but it didn't make her want to cry and fall to the ground anymore. At least that was progress.

"Because right now it's still my property. And I have to take care of it."

"Got it. Well, I'm here to help in whatever way I can. I will lend you my ample muscles for as long as you need them," he said, flexing them proudly with a smile on his face.

"I like this side of you." She didn't mean to say it out loud. She had been thinking it, but she certainly wasn't trying to get it to come out of her mouth.

"Really?"

"Yes, really. Today you don't seem like the uptight billionaire that you did when you first showed up here."

"I'll take that as a compliment," he said with a laugh.

They drove along for a while, just chatting about various things. It wasn't exactly an exciting drive but it took a good twenty minutes to get to Whiskey Ridge so they had to make the best of it. The winding roads made travel take a lot longer than in the city.

Jill liked driving into Whiskey Ridge as often as she could. The small town feel, complete with the town square, was just what she needed to make herself feel connected sometimes. There wasn't a lot in Whiskey Ridge either, but it was more than she had access to at The Retreat.

She loved going to the diner, the coffee shop and sometimes just sitting in the gazebo on the square watching people go by. She would always try to imagine what their lives were like, and that fed her creative imagination.

Winston actually lived in Whiskey Ridge and had for his whole life. His fondness for The Retreat originated from the fact that he had camped out in those mountains throughout his entire childhood and adulthood.

Jill pulled into the small parking lot of the only grocery store in town. It was a mom-and-pop place, and certainly not like a big chain grocery store. When she parked, she glanced at Patrick who was staring at the building with a slight smile on his face.

"What?"

"This is the grocery store?"

"Yes it is. It's not quite two-thousand square feet, but it's big by Whiskey Ridge standards."

"Wow. And you're sure we can get what we need in here? Maybe we should drive to the next big town."

"We can get what we need, Patrick. You'd be surprised at how little we need up here. Life doesn't have to be so complicated or expensive."

Jill opened her door and jumped down from the truck as Patrick did the same. They walked into the store, Patrick still looking around like he'd landed on Mars.

"Well, hello, Jill!" a rotund woman said as they walked in the door.

"Hey, Doris. How're you doing today?"

The woman pulled her into a tight hug. "Doing just fine. Coming down for some supplies?"

"You know it. Listen, how's your husband doing? Did he get over his knee surgery okay?"

"He did. But he's a big baby. Had me waiting on him hand and foot!"

Patrick stood there as the two women chatted for a few moments, obviously uncomfortable. For someone who had done so well in business, it struck Jill that he wasn't really good with interpersonal communication.

After Doris went back to her register, Jill grabbed a shopping cart and started walking through the store with Patrick walking closely beside her.

"You seem a little uncomfortable," she said, smiling over at him. He loosened up a bit.

"Is it that obvious?"

"To me it is. What's going on?"

"I don't know. Maybe I'm just used to the big city."

"So you don't like the small town atmosphere?"

He shrugged his shoulders. "It's not that. I guess I just feel like the spotlight is on me in situations like this. You know, in the city, you can sort of blend into the crowd. But in a small town, everybody's business is out on display. Or at least that's how it feels."

Jill chuckled. "No, that's a pretty good assessment."

As they rounded the corner into the produce section, Jill froze in place. She stared across a huge display of apples and couldn't believe her eyes. It was her sister. She seemed to be alone but was holding the hand of a little girl who had the cutest blonde curls. Just like their mother.

Jill was dumbfounded. Her sister was barely out of high school and apparently already had a child who was old enough to walk. A feeling of heartache shot through her chest as she realized she'd missed being an aunt to her niece.

Her sister, Jamie, looked up, obviously shocked herself. They both just stared at each other for a moment before Jamie's face changed into a slight smile. She tugged on her daughter's hand and took a couple of steps forward closer to Jill.

Patrick stopped and looked at Jill, obviously confused about what was happening, But he didn't say anything, seeming to sense that this was a tense situation.

"Jamie?"

"Hey, Jill. Long time no see."

Jill nodded toward the little girl. "Yes, it has been a long time. Is this your daughter?"

Jamie smiled down at the little girl. "Yes, this is Madison. She's eighteen months."

Jill's heart sank. Had it really been that long? It wasn't like she and her sister had ever been overly close given their age difference, but she had hoped that maybe things would change once they became adults. That maybe they would go shopping together and get married and have their children grow up together. That maybe they would break the chain of dysfunction that had held her family together for what seemed like generations.

But apparently that hope was lost. The look on her sister's face was enough to know that their mother had likely poisoned her mind against Jill.

"I didn't even know you were pregnant."

"How would you? You abandoned mom and me a long time ago."

"I didn't abandon you. You know that's not how it went down."

"Whatever, Jill. You've always had your own way of thinking about things. I hear that you have some kind of anxiety camp for people up in the mountains?"

Jill sighed. "That's not exactly how I would describe it, but yes I do help people with anxiety. Lord knows I grew up with it and had to learn how to survive on my own."

Jamie laughed sarcastically and rolled her eyes. "Always the victim. I guess some things never change."

"Hey, why don't you chill out a little bit?" Patrick suddenly said, stepping forward as if he was going to stand between Jill and her sister. Jill was shocked. Why was this guy standing up for her when he really didn't know anything about her or her past?

"Excuse me?" Jamie said, a snarl on her face.

"It's okay, Patrick."

"No, it's not. You don't deserve to be spoken to like this. For your information," he said, directing his comments straight at Jamie, "your sister helps a lot of people. She's a savvy businesswoman, and you should be proud to be related to her."

"Who are you anyway?" Jamie asked, irritated by his comments.

Patrick froze for a moment. "I'm her friend."

Jamie rolled her eyes again and started pulling her daughter back toward the shopping cart. "Well, obviously you don't know much about her. Good luck, Jill."

With that, she walked away, disappearing down the cereal aisle. Jill didn't know what to say or do. She stood there, her face red from embarrassment, hands shaking. Finally, Patrick turned to her and took both of her hands in his.

"She doesn't know what she's talking about. She has no idea who you are or what you've been through."

Again, Jill felt like he knew more about her than he was saying, but how? Right now, she didn't want to pull on that string. She just wanted to get her items and get the heck out of Whiskey Ridge. Her sanctuary of a town didn't seem safe anymore now that her sister was obviously living nearby.

"Thanks for trying to help, but some things can't be fixed."

"Believe me, I understand."

The look in his eyes told her that he really did understand. That there was more to his story than he was letting on. For that day, Jill had experienced as much emotional upset as she could handle, and she just wanted to go back to The Retreat.

Patrick couldn't stop thinking about what had happened at the grocery store. The ride home had been really quiet with Jill obviously thinking about the interaction she'd had with her long lost sister. He felt so bad for her. He knew exactly what it was like to not have your family there to support you. He had been abandoned, but in a totally different way.

When they got back to The Retreat, Jill had excused herself to go upstairs for a little while, obviously needing some space to deal with her emotions.

Patrick decided to help her by putting up the groceries. They had also stopped on the way home to pick up the pavers she needed for the garden area, so he threw on his most casual clothes and headed out to the yard.

As he worked, digging and clearing and smoothing over the dirt in preparation for the pavers, he thought about the first time he met her. A part of him was surprised that she still didn't recognize him, but shaggy hair and acne had apparently helped to maintain his incognito status.

This place really was beautiful. Even though he had been here against his will all those years ago, the beauty and majesty of the Blue Ridge Mountains hadn't been lost on him.

He stopped digging and wiped his brow. As he looked around, he had to admit that it was hard to imagine all of this land being cleared to make way for the resort. It was sad when progress collided with beauty.

But some things just had to be done. Someone was bound to do it at some point, so it might as well be him. At least that's what he was trying to tell himself.

"What are you doing?" He didn't have to turn around to know that it was Winston standing behind him, a stern tone to his voice. Even though Patrick was a billionaire and one of the richest men in the world, something about this old man made him tremble a bit.

"Well, Winston, I'm working in the garden," he said, an irritated tone in his voice. In reality, he was irritated at Jill's sister more than anything.

"Does Jill know you're out here messing with her garden?"

"Actually she doesn't. But she's had a rough afternoon and I'm just trying to do something to help her." Patrick turned back around and started working again. But Winston didn't go away. He was definitely not somebody who was easily intimidated. Patrick felt like he would never be ever be able to win over this man's approval if he had twenty lifetimes to do it.

"She had a rough afternoon? What did you do?" Now he could see Winston standing in his peripheral vision, his

RACHEL HANNA

arms crossed and his chest stuck out like he was ready to rumble.

Patrick chuckled, slamming the shovel into the ground where it stood beside him like a bodyguard.

"I didn't do anything to her. We went into town to pick up groceries and she had a not so pleasant run in with a person from her past."

"Oh yeah? And who was that?"

"Her long lost sister."

Winston's face changed. There was a mixture of irritation and sadness. "I imagine that didn't go so well."

"No, it didn't. Honestly, I would never hit a woman but that's the first time I had the urge to."

Surprisingly, that got a bit of a chuckle out of Winston. "I understand that. Jill has told me a lot about her mother and her sister and her evil stepfather."

The old man sat down on a tall tree stump next to the garden. "Well, I can tell you from personal experience today that Jill won't be invited to their Thanksgiving any time soon."

Winston shook his head. "I just don't get it. She's one of the best women I've ever known. Only tries to help people. And to be turned away by her family... Well, they don't know what they're missing. She's like a granddaughter to me. Maybe even a daughter."

"Well, I don't get it either. And I didn't like it."

Winston eyed him carefully. "What I don't get is, why are you still here?"

Boy, it hadn't taken long for Winston to get right back to the point of not liking him.

"I'm here because she asked me to stay. She wants to help me with my high blood pressure problems."

Winston almost smiled again but quickly stopped

himself. "That sounds like her. Even though you're here to take her land, she still wants to help you."

Patrick sighed. "I'm not trying to take her land. She's going to lose it regardless, unless something major happens to change that. I'm just here to see if it would be a good fit for my portfolio."

As soon as he said it, he realized how stupid and trite it sounded.

"Well, I do hope that you find what works for your portfolio. But meanwhile, I'm trying to protect Jill from getting hurt any more than she already has."

He turned and started walking back towards the cabin. "Hey, Winston?"

"Yeah?"

"I know it doesn't seem like it, but I've had Jill's best interests at heart for longer than you can imagine."

Winston grunted, nodded his head slightly and turned to walk in the house.

CHAPTER 8

Jill stared at herself in the foyer mirror. She could see how tired she was. And seeing her sister in the grocery store had only added stress to her already full plate of it.

Worse than that was that she felt so embarrassed in front of Patrick. What must he think of her? And why did she even care?

Her mind was a whirlwind lately, which was a real problem since she was supposed to be teaching him how to reduce his stress. At least that would get a little bit easier today now that Alice and Ingrid would be leaving. Winston had chosen to stay until Patrick left, probably in an effort to protect her from some perceived threat.

For the next several days, she would be sharing her home with two men who seemed to be at odds for no particular reason. Winston was like an overprotective grandfather to her, and she had to admit she kind of liked it. Having no real family of her own anymore, Winston served as someone in her life who would give her real advice and stand beside her no matter what.

But she knew he was getting on in years. He wouldn't be

around forever, and then she would be dreadfully alone yet again. No husband, no boyfriend, no prospects. No kids to keep her busy. And no sister, obviously. Even though she had a mother out there somewhere, it was obvious that Jill wasn't a priority to her as she hadn't reached out in many years.

Yes, she was definitely feeling sorry for herself today. A good night of sleep had done nothing for her mood. She had just gone through the motions since her trip to the grocery store with Patrick the day before. Even dinner was a much quieter affair that night, with Winston regaling them with stories of his hiking adventures in the mountains surrounding The Retreat as a kid. Patrick watched him, but said nothing. It was almost as if he wanted to give some kind of input, but he was far too scared of Winston to do so.

Jill smiled slightly as she thought about the fact that this young man was scared of a senior citizen who used a cane to walk.

"Good morning," Patrick said from behind her. For some reason, seeing him made her feel a little better instantly. She was starting to grow comfortable with him being around. It made no logical sense, of course. He was only there for his own financial benefit. But just having another person around about her age gave her some kind of normalcy.

"Good morning. Breakfast is in the kitchen if you want something. I made some scrambled eggs and bacon this morning. Nothing overly exciting, but it will do the trick." She continued looking in the mirror, finally pulling her hair up into a high ponytail.

"Thanks. That should be plenty. So what's the plan for today?"

"Well, Ingrid and Alice are leaving, so there's no class

this morning. But I was thinking about taking another hike if you're game?"

"Is there more to see?"

Jill turned around, smiling. "There's always more to see. The landscape here changes every day."

"I'm not sure that's true, but I'm willing to take a gamble and see if you're right."

Jill laughed. "Well you don't have much of a choice. You agreed to follow my instructions, and you have several days left."

"I guess it's a little bit like being married," he said, without thinking, obviously.

"I wouldn't know."

"Neither would I."

They both laughed. "I'll pack a few things and we'll be on our way. Meet me on the porch in about half an hour?

"It's a date," he said.

Jill turned to go up the stairs, hoping he didn't see the smile on her face. She hadn't heard the word "date" in a very long time. And this definitely wasn't a date, but something inside of her almost wanted it to be.

As they trekked through the woods and up some challenging hills, Patrick felt the need to find out more about how Jill's life had been since he last saw her on the bridge.

"So, did you go to school around here?"

"No. We actually lived a little closer to Atlanta in a northern suburb."

"Did you like it? I mean school?"

"No, it wasn't my favorite thing. I was bullied pretty relentlessly."

Patrick glanced at her. He had a very hard time believing that anyone would bully her. She was so beautiful and kind and smart and funny. What in the world could they focus on that was a negative?

"Why were you bullied?"

"Why is anyone bullied really? People didn't like who I was."

"But you're so..."

Jill stopped and turned to him. "I'm so what?"

He smiled. "Well, at the risk of sounding very surface level, you're beautiful. Maybe they were just jealous?"

Jill smiled, and he could've sworn that her face turned a little red. "Well, thank you, Patrick. Believe me, that means a lot coming from you."

"I'm not as bad as you might think."

She smiled slightly. "I don't actually think you're bad. I think you're misunderstood, even by me sometimes."

He'd been misunderstood most of his life. "So do you think they were jealous?"

She started walking again, so he followed.

"No. I was bullied every year of school because of the color of my eyes."

This time, Patrick stopped in his tracks. "You've got to be kidding me." It was only then that he remembered her saying that on the bridge that day.

"I'm not kidding. I was called all kinds of names from the time I entered school until the time I left." She dropped her backpack and reached into it for bottle of water, taking a long sip.

"But your eyes are so..."

"Spooky? Weird? Ghostly?"

Patrick stared into her eyes for a moment. "Gorgeous. Wise. Deep vessels of blue that I could get lost in for hours."

He heard Jill's breath catch in her throat. They just stood there, staring at each other for a few moments. It should've been awkward, but it wasn't. For a moment, he worried that she was finally going to recognize him.

"I don't know what to say..."

"You don't have to say anything. But just know that if you ever point out one of those bullies to me when we're in public, take my wallet before they cart me off to jail because I'm going to need bail money."

Jill broke out into laughter. It was the first time he had really seen her without her walls up. Within moments, she was laughing so hard that tears were streaming down her face."

"See? I can be funny occasionally."

"I think you're funny more often than you think," she said. "We better keep moving before I lose my motivation."

They continued walking and talking, with Patrick being very careful to avoid any conversations that talked about his own childhood. Every time she seemed to be ready to ask him some questions, he thought of another one for her.

"We've been walking a long time. Is there a destination you have in mind?"

"Well, actually, I am a wee bit... lost."

Patrick stopped. "Are you serious? Please tell me you're not serious."

Jill gritted her teeth together and shrugged. "I'm sorry, but I've never been up in this area before. It's just that we got to talking and I lost track of where we were... I was actually enjoying your company."

"Well, as shocking as that is, don't you think we should figure out where we are?"

Jill looked around, craning her head from one side to the other. "I have absolutely no idea. I mean we could try to follow the same path back down but I know we made a couple of turns... I don't know if we're even on my property anymore."

Patrick tried not to get upset. He had really enjoyed spending this time with her so the last thing he wanted to do was start an argument.

"Okay, it should be easy to use the GPS on your phone."

Her eyes widened. "I didn't bring my phone."

Now he was really having a hard time not getting frustrated. "You didn't bring your phone? But you always have your phone."

"I know but I figured since I was sort of riding you about not bringing your phone that I shouldn't bring mine..."

Patrick looked around, trying to figure out what to do. All they had was a backpack with some snacks and water. They were at the top of a mountain, yet he couldn't see The Retreat anywhere in his view. It was an hour until nightfall, extremely cold and they were apparently completely lost.

"Okay, then we need to make some decisions. We only have about an hour until the sun goes down, and we definitely don't need to be walking around on this mountain. We could try heading down but if we go the wrong direction, that could be pretty dangerous."

"So what are you suggesting?"

Patrick sucked in a deep breath and then slowly blew it out. "I think we're going to have to make camp for the night."

"You want to camp overnight? Out here? But it's freezing cold and..." As if on cue, snowflakes started falling over head.

"Oh great. Isn't it a little bit early in the season for this?"

Jill caught some snowflakes on her glove. "Apparently not."

RACHEL HANNA

~

Jill was so embarrassed. Here she was trying to help him reduce his stress level and somehow she had managed to get both of them lost on the mountain, just before dark, snow falling. Maybe she should close up her business for the safety of the public.

So far, he had been nice about it, but he didn't have much choice anyway. They had very little time before it was going to get dark, and they somehow needed to get a fire going or they were going to freeze to death. Why hadn't she brought her phone?

"Okay, I think I've gathered enough wood. Thank goodness we found this outcropping of rocks. I think it will protect us from a lot of the wind."

"For a city boy, you seem to know a lot about camping."

"I think pretty much anyone knows to gather wood and find a place to sleep. Don't be so impressed."

She couldn't tell if he was mad at her or just a little bit terrified. Either way, his tone was growing short with her.

Jill propped her backpack up on one of the rocks and reached inside in an effort to see what snacks she had packed. She had done everything in such a rush that she honestly couldn't remember what they had.

This backpack had been with her for so many years. She used to take it out when she would go hiking with early visitors to The Retreat.

"I think I have a first aid kit in here," she said to no one in particular.

"Well let's hope that we don't need it," Patrick said with a laugh.

She opened the various zippers, shoving her hand down in all the crevices of the bag . When her hand touched upon something she forgot she had, she giggled with delight.

"Oh my gosh!"

"What?" Patrick asked, walking a step closer to her. She pulled her hand out of the bag to reveal a flint. "Now we can start a fire!"

Patrick let out a relieved breath. "Thank God. Why didn't you tell me you had that?"

"Because I didn't know."

"Go figure. I don't know why I should be surprised. I've never known a woman who didn't have a plethora of strange items in her purse."

Jill rolled her eyes. "This isn't my purse."

She handed him the flint, and he went to work on starting the fire. Within a few minutes, they had a large enough flame to create smoke signals if they wanted to.

Patrick walked around, gathering pine straw that he dug up from under the surface of the forest floor. The top section was wet, so he had to find whatever dry straw he could for them to sleep on. Jill didn't think they would be getting much sleep anyway. It was freezing cold, incredibly dark and the fire would need to be stoked throughout the long night they had ahead of them.

As they sat down on the bed of pine straw, Jill sighed.

"Patrick, I am so sorry for all of this. It was my responsibility to keep you safe out here, and I let you down."

He knocked his shoulder into hers. "Don't beat yourself up. I should've been paying attention too. I was just so mesmerized by our conversation."

She pulled her knees up to her chest, hugging them for warmth. "I have to say that I didn't see this coming."

"Getting lost in the woods?"

"No. This unlikely... friendship?"

Patrick chuckled. "So we're friends?"

"Maybe. Tonight. But when you own this property and I don't, I can't promise that I'm going to feel exactly like you're my friend."

"At least if we're friends, you can come visit anytime you want."

"Yeah. I guess there's that."

Jill reached her hand into the bag and pulled out a couple of bags of chips and an extra water bottle. She opened it up, taking a sip and then handing it to him. They sat and ate the chips, staring into the flickering flames as they rose and disappeared into the darkness.

"I really wish I had worn my thicker coat," Jill said. Although the fire was large, it wasn't doing a whole lot to keep her from feeling the freezing cold temperatures. She could only get so close to the fire without incinerating herself.

Patrick scooted over closer and wrapped one arm around her shoulder. "Is this okay?"

She immediately felt the warmth of his body against hers. It was nice and something she hadn't experienced in a very long time. "Yes, it's fine."

They sat that way for a very long time, no words spoken between them. As the night crept on, Jill started to get sleepy. Her head fell, and landed on his shoulder, waking her up.

"Try to stay awake. I think you're getting tired from the cold."

"Probably so. I just wish there was a way we could get warmer."

"Wait here." Patrick stood up, and walked into the darkness. For a moment, she was frightened but then figured there probably weren't many wild animals out roaming around in the cold. Thankfully, it only flurried for a while and then let up.

A few minutes later, she heard noises. Patrick appeared from the darkness, dragging large pieces of wood and logs with him.

"What are you doing?"

He dropped one of the trunks and grinned. "I'm building you a house."

She watched him work for several minutes, dragging big trunks, pieces of wood and limbs from the dark forest. She offered to help, but he would have none of it.

He built up the side of the shelter where the wind was coming in until it was taller than Jill's head. Suddenly, the wind couldn't touch her anymore. The warmth of the fire penetrated the small area and she could feel her feet again.

When he finally sat back down, he was out of breath and shivering. This time, she wrapped her arms around him, rubbing her hands up and down his arms in an effort to warm him up.

"You're quite the builder, Patrick."

"Surprising, huh?"

Who knew that spending hours on the side of a freezing cold mountain could be so enjoyable? But here he sat, next to a woman he'd known since he was fifteen years old, enjoying every second of conversation with her.

And being pressed up against her didn't hurt. Fire or not, they needed the extra heat, and he wasn't complaining. Having her cuddled up by his side felt more right than he wanted to admit.

"I was going to jump."

"What?"

"I was going to jump," Jill repeated.

"I don't understand..."

"When I was at the bridge... as a kid... I went there to jump. That's why it's such an important place to me."

Patrick stilled. He didn't know what to say. Of course, he already knew this information, but he didn't want her to think that he did. He didn't want to under react. He didn't want to overreact. This was one of the first times in his life where he had absolutely no idea what to say.

Thankfully, she continued. "I was going through a really rough time in my life. My mother married a man who was not a good person. He was pretty abusive, at least verbally, to me. But at least I still had some of my mother's attention until she got pregnant with my sister a few months after they married. Things went downhill really fast. I was the black sheep of the family. My mom didn't spend any time with me and they both were so engrossed with my sister that I was getting lost in the mix. On top of that, he made me feel terrible about myself any chance he got. My mother always sided with him. Anyway, we ended up out here on a family camping trip. And then there was the bullying at school. My mother said I was being a baby about it, to get a thicker skin, and so on. Things came to a head, and I just couldn't deal with it anymore. So I ended up on the bridge."

Instinctively, Patrick reached over and took her hand. She smiled gratefully.

"I never talk about it. I don't think I've ever told anyone what happened that day. But there was this kid, about my age. He just showed up on the bridge like some kind of adolescent angel. He was kind of a jerk at first," she said. Patrick couldn't help but chuckle. Jill looked at him, confused.

"Sorry. I just thought it was funny that he was a jerk. I think most boys are when they're that age."

"Yeah, I guess so. Anyway, I don't even know what he was doing there or where his family was, but he spoke to me. He talked me out of making a stupid decision that I couldn't take back. And the reality was that I had never planned to jump before. It was a spur of the moment thing when I saw the bridge in the distance, and I'm so glad that he stopped me. I never forgot him. I wish I could go back and say thank you."

"So you never saw him again?"

"No. Honestly, he kissed me and then ran off into the woods. I guess it doesn't say much for my kissing skills," she said laughing.

Patrick shook his head. "I'm sure it had nothing to do with that."

"Well, whatever the case, I never saw him again. I wanted to. I wish I had asked his last name or something. To be honest, I've tried even searching his first name on social media, which was a fool's errand, but it was something. I often scan the faces of men that I see walking through Whiskey Ridge, hoping that maybe he has visited the area again as an adult. I would love to see him and be able to say thank you."

For a moment, Patrick considered telling her. He thought about the look on her face when he would tell her who he really was. But then he stopped himself. He had gotten so far into this whole thing that telling her now would only make her hate him. And the thought of her hating him was too much to bear.

"That's why the bridge is so important to me. Not only did my life change that day, but I met an amazing person there. I guess in the back of my mind, I think as long as the bridge is there, I might see him again one day. Probably sounds silly to you," she said, looking at him.

"Not silly at all."

"I sometimes wonder if he ever thought about me after that day."

Patrick smiled. "I'm absolutely sure he did."

She cocked her head to the side. "Oh yeah? And why is that?"

"Because you're an impossible woman to forget, Jill." Without thinking, he pressed his lips to the top of her head.

She looked up at him, her eyes soft and sleepy. Patrick found himself unable to think clearly when she looked at him. He wanted to kiss her worse than he wanted to take his next breath, but instead he settled for her forehead, pressing his lips there next. His hand cradled the side of her face as she stared at him, probably wondering what in the world he was doing. Or maybe she was remembering him.

"I'm sorry," he said, dropping his hand away from her face.

"Don't be," she said softly. "I'm not."

She snuggled up close to him again, laying her head on his shoulder, and Patrick felt like his world had just turned upside down.

CHAPTER 9

As soon as the sun rose, Patrick and Jill started trying to make their way down the mountain. There was no talk about what had happened the night before. No mention of the kiss on her forehead or the obvious attraction they'd both felt. Instead, Patrick seemed to be back to business as usual, and she'd managed to get her feelings back in check enough to get them to safety.

It took a lot longer than she expected, but eventually The Retreat came into view after a couple of hours of walking in every direction.

As big as the area was, Jill was surprised they found their way back at all. It would be easy to get lost for days or weeks in the Blue Ridge Mountains.

"Well, I guess we can call it an adventure," she said with a laugh as they made their way onto the screen porch.

Before Patrick could respond, Winston came flying through the doorway. Well, he was walking as fast as an eighty-something-year-old with a limp could walk.

"Where in the world have you two been? I was up all

night, worried sick. I was just about to call the rescue squad."

"I'm so sorry, Winston. We decided to go for a hike yesterday. Somehow, I got us turned around and we couldn't find our way back down the mountain before the sun went down."

"You mean to tell me that the two of you camped in the woods last night, in the freezing cold, without any supplies?"

Patrick nodded. "Thankfully, Jill had a flint in her backpack. So we built a fire and just made it through the night as best we could."

Winston looked irritated and relieved. "I'm glad y'all made it. Next time don't go out without your cell phone," he said before turning around and slowly heading back up the stairs.

"I feel so guilty. Poor Winston," she said.

"I would apologize to him but I don't think it would mean very much coming from me," Patrick said with a laugh.

Before Jill could respond, they both heard the front door open. She wasn't expecting any guests to check in, so she walked into the foyer to see who was coming into her house.

The young man, probably in his mid-twenties, was standing in her entryway wearing a very nice suit. In fact, it reminded her of Patrick showing up just a few days ago looking much the same.

"Excuse me. I'm looking for Patrick Scott."

Before Jill could call for him, Patrick came around the corner. He stopped in his tracks when he saw the man, his mouth hanging open.

"Derrick? What on Earth are you doing here?"

Derrick stepped forward and shook Patrick's hand. "I've been trying to reach you for a couple of days. You never go offline like this. Why aren't you answering your cell phone?

"I, uh, decided to take some time off this week. I'm sort of living an unplugged lifestyle right now." He glanced at Jill, a slight smile on his face. "So why are you here again?"

Derrick looked around the room. "Well, I wanted to see this place, for one thing. The bank called and gave me the information, so I thought I'd take a drive up here and check it out and see if I could find you. It's kind of... out here."

Patrick chuckled. "Yes, it's a good ways out, but it's a beautiful property. Oh, Derrick let me introduce you to Jill. She owns The Retreat."

Jill didn't crack a smile, but did manage to extend her hand. "Nice to meet you."

"Nice to meet you too."

"So, how exactly do you to know each other?" Jill asked.

"Derrick is one of my business partners in this whole conference center deal."

Jill was confused. Patrick was a billionaire. Why did he need a business partner?

"Oh. I didn't think you had business partners given your... financial status."

Derrick laughed out loud. "Trust me, he's doing me a favor. Trying to help me get started in this commercial real estate world. He doesn't need me in the slightest."

"That's not true. Derrick has a great mind for business. Sometimes he helps me make decisions that are difficult to make. He's very good at being objective."

Jill wasn't sure what that meant. "Well, I'm pretty tired so I think I'm going to go upstairs and take a nap before I need to prepare lunch. You two enjoy your visit," she said as she walked toward the stairs.

"Hey, Jill?" Patrick called after her.

"Yeah?"

"I had a nice time on our hike," he said, winking at her. For the first time since she had seen the mystery figure on the bridge all those years ago, Jill suddenly had butterflies in her stomach. This was getting way too complicated.

~

"I'm just trying to picture you out in the freezing cold weather all night long acting like some kind of mountain man," Derrick said with a laugh.

"I'm a lot handier in the outdoors than you might imagine," Patrick said. "So tell me what you're really doing here. I left word that I was going off-line for a few days before I did it."

The two men stopped at an overlook. "I'm just a little worried about you, man. I've never seen you stop working for so long. I thought I better come up here and make sure you still had your head on straight."

"Why would you think I didn't?"

Derrick laughed. "Because this is very out of character for you, Patrick. Is there something going on with you and this woman?"

Patrick rolled his eyes. "Do you honestly think I would let something like this come between me and this conference center deal? You know me better than that. I don't get tied up in personal relationships when it comes to business."

Even as Patrick said it, he knew it was a lie. He had been trying everything in his mind to convince himself to step away from this deal almost since the moment he got there. But that seemed too dangerous. That felt like giving in. The last time he believed in somebody, he got the short end of the stick.

"Okay, if you say so, then I have to believe you. This deal is going to be one for the books. I hope you aren't backing out."

Patrick shook his head. "I don't back out on business deals. You should know that. I think you came all the way out here for nothing."

"No, I didn't. I still would like to see the property. So are you going to show me around or what?"

After walking around for an hour, Derrick was more than ready to go back to The Retreat. Plus, it was almost lunchtime, so Patrick had no problem heading back there himself. His stomach was growling something fierce after missing breakfast.

They walked onto the screen porch and sat down in a couple of rocking chairs. Patrick didn't know where Jill was, although he assumed that she was back in the kitchen working on lunch. She really didn't need to do that since it was just the two of them and Winston staying at the place, but she was a dedicated hostess, nonetheless.

"So, are you expecting to stay here tonight?" Patrick asked. "Because if so, I'd like to pay Jill a little something extra for your room."

"No. Actually, I have an early meeting tomorrow. That Savannah deal is looking like it might go through, so I need to head back to the office and try to hold it together. Dealing with Donovan can be challenging sometimes, you know."

Just hearing the details of another business deal made Patrick cringe a bit. He had to admit that he'd enjoyed being unplugged the last few days, completely focusing on spending time with Jill and looking at the beautiful surroundings. He was going to be sad when he had to leave and go back to his gray office walls and slightly boring life.

"Well, at least have some lunch with us before you head out."

"Sounds like a plan. But before we do that, I do have a couple of questions about this property. Actually, I have an idea to throw out at you."

Patrick leaned forward. The last thing he wanted was for Jill to hear him talking about plans for her property. She was already sad enough that she was going to lose it, and he didn't want to rub it in.

"Okay. What kind of idea?"

"Well, I've been thinking about that bridge we saw. It's nice and all. I know you want to preserve it, but I'm thinking that putting a state-of-the-art zip line course in that area would be a major attraction and a money maker."

Patrick leaned back in his chair. "No. I'm not tearing down that bridge. "

"Patrick, come on. I don't know what your attachment is to that old thing, but we've got to get it out of there. It doesn't go with the rest of the plans for the conference center."

"I told you that I'm not negotiable about this."

"Even if you can add thousands of dollars a month to the bottom line?"

Patrick rolled his eyes. "This is one of those times when I'm going to point out my billionaire status. Thousands of extra dollars a month doesn't really get me motivated, Derrick."

Worried that they were talking too loud, Patrick stood up and motioned for Derrick to follow him outside. As they approached the door, Derrick patted him on the shoulder.

"You know I'm right. That bridge has to come down. It's

right in the middle of everything, and having that zip line course is important. It will be a great attraction for this entire area and bring a lot of money to your future employees and the surrounding town."

"I get what you're saying..."

"Then you need to trust me. Getting rid of that bridge will make way for something even better. Right now, it's just an old remnant of the past that isn't serving any real purpose."

"But Jill..."

Derrick squeezed Patrick's shoulder. "Look, man, you said it yourself. I help you make tough decisions because I'm objective. The bridge needs to go. Don't get all mixed up in emotions here."

Patrick looked at the doorway to make sure no one had heard their conversation. "Come on, let's take this outside."

Jill couldn't believe what she'd just heard. As she had come around the corner to offer sandwiches to Derrick and Patrick, she never expected to hear the tail end of their conversation.

But her ears perked up when she heard them speaking about the bridge. Derrick was urging Patrick to tear it down and make way for some zip line course. And from what she could hear, Patrick wasn't exactly arguing with him.

He'd been lying to her. Apparently, he'd had no intention of keeping the bridge at all. Instead, he was going to destroy it – and her memories along with it – just for rich people to be able to fly through the forest.

Her stomach churned. How could she have been so stupid as to think that this super wealthy guy would have any interest in keeping the bridge? It was all about money for him. She felt so ridiculous for believing that she was somehow changing his mind or helping him reduce his stress. Or that he was developing feelings for her.

The Retreat was going to be gone. She was going to be without a business, without a job, without a life. And now, the one place on Earth that made her feel hopeful was going to be torn down in the process.

It all broke her heart.

"Hey there, young lady. Everything okay?" Winston asked from the doorway. Jill was sitting at the kitchen table, her head in her hands.

"I don't know anymore. Why does life have to be so incredibly complicated?"

Winston sat down across from her and reached over to pat her hand. "Because it's life. That's how it's supposed to be. Otherwise, it'd be boring, right?"

"Well, I'm not so sure. Why does it seem so easy for some people and so difficult for others?"

"Sweetie, sometimes we make it more difficult than it has to be."

"Agreed. But sometimes other people are the ones making the mess that you can't clean up."

"This must be about Patrick?"

"Yes, in a way. I let my guard down, and I shouldn't have."

Winston cleared his throat. "I'm not so sure about that."

"Wait. Are you actually defending him?"

"Not exactly. I just think maybe there's more to him than meets the eye."

"I can't believe what I'm hearing. I thought you couldn't stand him?"

"He's growing on me. Slightly."

"Well, I learned my lesson. He'll be leaving soon, and

this place will be a part of my history. As sad as I'll be, I'm ready to see what the rest of my life has in store."

"That's a good way to look at it, but don't write this place off just yet. I have a feeling that it holds more miracles for you, young lady."

Winston stood up and started walking to the door. "Don't you want a sandwich for lunch?"

"No thanks. I'm actually going into town to have a little lunch. Sometimes, we need a change in scenery to see things in a new light. Try it sometime."

Jill laughed. "I had plenty of scenery last night when I was stuck in the woods. I think I'll stay here where it's safe."

Jill stood in the middle of the screened porch, the only place on the property where she could get a panoramic view of the land she loved so much. She turned slowly, trying to take in as much of the scenery as she could. Before long, she wouldn't have this view anymore. She'd probably have some crappy one bedroom apartment overlooking a dumpster.

Okay, maybe she was letting her feelings get away with her.

Her heart jumped in her chest as she waited for Patrick to come back from talking to Derrick outside. Now that she knew he was just conning her, telling her what she wanted to hear, she wanted to get rid of him as soon as possible.

But how would she explain why she wanted him to leave? The last thing she wanted was for him to know that he had gotten to her. She wanted to keep at least a shred of her dignity, whatever she had left of it.

"Oh, hey, Jill. I was just about to walk Derrick to his car. Unfortunately, he can't stay for lunch after all."

There he stood, a big smile on his face. What thoughts must be running through his mind? Was he pleased with himself? Maybe lying to a woman who was in financial straits somehow gave him a thrill? The whole thing made her sick.

"Sorry to hear that. Have a good trip back." With that, Jill turned and walked upstairs without looking back. The last thing she wanted was for him to know that he was affecting her. She was going to get through the next few days without interacting with Patrick as much as possible. And then, she would start her life over, mindful of the fact she really couldn't trust anyone in the world. Not her sister. Not her banker. And certainly not Patrick.

Patrick was confused. After spending the night in the woods with Jill, he thought they were making some progress. He was starting to develop stronger feelings for her, a fact which he was having a harder time ignoring by the moment. But when he came back with Derrick from their chat outside, she was different. Standoffish. Angry, perhaps?

He tried to figure out what he had done. But he couldn't think of anything. Maybe Winston had filled her head with something? But that didn't seem possible since he hadn't done anything terribly wrong that he could think of.

He was fairly sure that she hadn't heard his talk with Derrick. They walked pretty far from the property to discuss his plans for The Retreat and the bridge. In fact, their conversation had gotten heated a couple of times which was why Derrick decided not to stay for lunch.

But right now, Patrick just wanted to figure out what was

going on with Jill. Like a man going straight into the lion's den, he walked up the stairs and knocked on her door.

After a few moments, she swung open the door, her bright blue eyes looking up at him like she could shoot daggers straight through his head.

"Hey. I just wanted to come up and check on you. You seemed a little upset downstairs. Is everything okay?"

She shook her head slightly, looked at the floor and chuckled. "Yes, everything is perfectly fine. My life is going exactly as I had planned." She stared up at him, no hint of a smile on her face. Yep, she was ticked off about something. He just didn't have any idea what it was.

"all right... Is there anything I can do?"

"No, Patrick, there's nothing you can do. But listen, I think I've given you just about as much of my time as I have available. Obviously, I need to focus on getting this place packed up so I can move soon."

He stood there, staring at her for a moment. She was giving up? This wasn't like her at all. He was supposed to stay a few more days, but was she asking him to leave?

"I don't understand... I thought you wanted me to stay here..."

"Well, if there's one thing I've learned in the last week, it's that things can change very quickly. I'd appreciate it if you would make your way back to the city as soon as possible. I'll be glad to refund you a prorated amount for your stay." Patrick had paid her the going rate for someone staying a full week.

"No, that's okay. I wanted you to have that money," he said, his stomach churning.

"Suit yourself. I won't really have time to work with you on your stress anymore, but I would highly recommend seeing someone in your area."

With that, she slowly shut the door in his face and Patrick was left to wonder what in the world had just happened.

~

Jill's hands were shaking. Her stomach was nauseous, and her heart was racing faster than she had ever remembered, including that one time she decided to run a half marathon without much training. She'd ended up vomiting in the bushes about eight miles in, and her friend had to carry her to the car. Not her finest moment, for sure.

Looking at Patrick, the confusion on his face, almost made her heart ache. If she wasn't so incredibly mad at him, she might have felt bad.

But this wasn't a misunderstanding. She knew what she had heard. And no matter how much she found herself attracted to him, he wasn't who she thought he was. He knew what that bridge meant to her, and he'd made a promise that he was apparently intent on breaking.

And now, she was left with the realization that she was going to lose The Retreat and the bridge. The rug was definitely going to get ripped out from under her, and there wasn't anything she could do about it.

Sometimes, giving in and letting go is the best thing you can do for yourself, she thought.

So, she decided that she would call the bank and give the deed back as soon as possible. She needed to rip this place off of her like a Band-Aid. It was apparently time to move on with her life, whether she liked it or not.

CHAPTER 10

Jill hadn't come back out of her room by the time Patrick was ready to leave. He lingered around in the entryway, hoping that she would come down and at least say goodbye. But she didn't. And he still didn't really understand why.

His heart told him to go talk to her until she admitted what was wrong. But his head was telling him to just let it go. No matter what, this wasn't going to end well. She had made their break much cleaner. His brain was telling him to get in his car, drive straight back to the city and never look back.

But he couldn't stop himself. There was still a part of him that thought of her as that fifteen-year-old girl who needed his help on the bridge that day.

He slowly walked down the hall and stood outside of her door. After a few moments of working up his courage, he lightly knocked. At first, she didn't answer. But when he knocked again, he heard her sigh.

"Jill? I was getting ready to leave and I would really like to tell you goodbye."

"Goodbye," she said softly. He could tell she was standing

just on the other side of the door, the shadow of her feet breaking up the light underneath it.

"So you're not even going to open the door?"

"Look, Patrick, I think it's best that I don't. I'm ready to cut my losses and get on with my life. I'll give the bank a call so that you can get your hands on this property as soon as possible."

Now he really was confused. The fight that had been in her the whole time was gone suddenly. Nothing made any sense.

"Jill, is something wrong? Let me help you."

"You can't help me. I can only help myself at this point. Please, just go, Patrick."

He stepped back and stared at the closed door. There was nothing more that he could do, so he decided to go ahead and leave The Retreat and try not to think about the woman he was leaving behind.

As Jill packed her last box, memories of owning The Retreat flew through her head. She was going to miss this place so much. It was like losing her child. It had been the only thing that had held her together for the last few years, and the feeling of her dreams dying was as soul crushing as she imagined it would be.

Saying goodbye to Winston had been one of the hardest things she'd ever had to do. For a moment, more like a fleeting second, she had considered staying in Whiskey Ridge but the memories would just be too hard.

She couldn't imagine sitting in the town square, having a cup of coffee, watching tourists drive up to the conference center that used to be part of her property. And if she ever saw someone zip lining where the bridge once stood, she couldn't be responsible for what she might do. Thoughts of getting a giant pair of scissors, like out of a Saturday morning cartoon, and cutting the line danced through her head.

Instead, she had decided to move clear across the country to get a fresh start. She found a small spa in Colorado that was looking for a new yoga teacher. It wasn't her dream job, especially after having owned her own business for so long, but it would be a paycheck and a new beginning. She desperately needed both right now.

She was only taking her personal possessions with her on the long drive across the country, so thankfully a moving van wasn't necessary. But she was a bit worried about her old truck making such a long drive.

After loading up the last of her boxes, she looked back up at the cabin that had been her home and her dream for the last three years. A sense of gratitude mixed with loss almost overwhelmed her as her eyes filled with tears. Nothing would ever be the same.

For a moment, she considered hiking to the bridge to say a final goodbye to the place that had changed her life, but she just couldn't bring herself to do it. It was too final, too hard. The memories she had would have to feed her heart for a lifetime.

She climbed up into her truck, slammed the heavy door and drove off down the dirt road, watching The Retreat disappear in her rearview mirror.

It had been two weeks since Patrick had left The Retreat, and he was still no closer to understanding what had happened with Jill. Even though he didn't want to admit it to himself, he'd had thoughts about building a life with her one day. Thoughts that scared him to the core of his soul.

But the way she'd pushed him away so suddenly only reminded him of why he didn't do relationships. Feelings and emotions were a lot more dangerous than bad business deals. Money didn't have the ability to hurt people like feelings did.

Today, whether he liked it or not, he was being forced to be reminded of what had happened because he was back in Whiskey Ridge to sign off on the final plans for the property at a local attorney's office. He'd found out that mountain people were different, and they sure didn't want to travel into the big city to sign paperwork. If he ever wanted to get this plan approved, he had to go back up to the place he thought he'd never go to again.

"Coffee. Black," he said to the barista at the small coffee shop on the square. The long drive had done nothing for his fatigue. Sleepless nights weren't a new thing for him, and now he tossed and turned a lot thinking about Jill. Where was she? Was she okay?

"Well, I'll be a monkey's uncle," he heard from behind him. No mistaking that voice. It was Winston.

"Hey there, Winston. How are you?" Patrick asked, reaching out his hand. Winston's grip was a lot firmer than one might imagine.

"Pretty good. What're you doing up here?" Always right to the point, Patrick thought to himself.

"Just have some final papers to get signed."

Winston waved for him to sit down at a nearby table. Patrick really wanted to get to the attorney's office, but he took a seat anyway.

"So, have you heard from Jill lately?"

Patrick chuckled. "No. Jill doesn't want to talk to me anymore."

"Oh yeah? And why is that?"

"I don't know, Winston. Why don't you tell me?" He eyed the old man carefully.

Winston grunted and raised his bushy eyebrows. "Son, I don't have the foggiest notion of what you did."

"Excuse me? Why do you think I did something?"

"Because that woman had feelings for you."

"Why do you say that?"

"Because I have eyes. They may not be so good anymore, but I have 'em. Anyone could see something was brewing with you two."

"Well, it isn't brewing anymore."

"She was upset."

"Upset? About what?"

Winston looked up, as if he was trying to remember something. "All I know is she was real upset after you went outside with your friend. Said something about life being complicated and that she shouldn't have let her guard down."

Patrick was more confused than ever. "I just don't get it."

"Did you say anything that maybe she overheard?"

"I don't think... Wait a minute! Oh my gosh... She must have overheard Derrick urging me to tear down the bridge."

"The bridge? You can't do that. It means a lot to her."

"I know that. I told her I wouldn't, but then Derrick was trying to convince me. I didn't want to upset her, so I took that conversation outside."

"I bet she thought you lied to her."

Patrick looked at Winston. "Why are you trying to help me figure this out? I mean, you haven't exactly been my biggest fan."

"Because I love Jill, and if you make her happy, then I'm happy."

"I'm not so sure I make her happy."

"You could."

Patrick thought for a moment. "Say, Winston, would you be willing to help me?"

"Depends on what it is..."

"Do you happen to know how to get in touch with Jill?"

Jill stood at the place she thought she'd never stand again. It had taken Winston a lot of convincing to get her to come back to the bridge, but when he'd told her that he wanted to say a final goodbye to her and bring her an important gift, she couldn't refuse. He was her only family at this point, after all, and she didn't have anyone else who cared about her like he did.

But he was late, and she was getting antsy. She wanted to get off the bridge as soon as possible. Her job in Colorado started in a few days, and she was ready to get out of the dingy motel she'd been staying in since leaving The Retreat.

As she'd driven back up the driveway, her heart felt like it was going to shatter into a million pieces. Saying goodbye to this place a second time felt like it would be harder. She'd had days to think about her losses, including Patrick. Losing him had been almost as hard as losing her business and her property. But he wasn't who she thought he was.

"Come on, Winston," she whispered as she stared out over the blue colored mountains.

"Hey," she heard a voice say from behind her. Jill froze in place when she realized it was Patrick. What was he doing here? She slowly turned around.

"Why are you here?" She wanted to be angry, but seeing him again only made her feel warm inside... and that made her mad at herself.

"To see you."

"Wait... Where's Winston?"

"Sitting at a nice warm coffee shop on the square."

She sucked in a sharp breath and shook her head. "You two worked together to get me here? Why?"

"You know, Jill, I tend to think of life as a series of tests."

"What?" she asked, confused.

"Like a video game."

"I don't... Wait. Someone said that to me before. Did I tell you about that guy? On the bridge? That he said that to me?" She was wracking her brain trying to remember their previous conversations.

"No."

"Then how did you..." She stared at him for a long moment, her mind racing. Then, like something out of a movie, she flashed back to that day and saw him as clear as day. No shaggy hair, no random adolescent pimples, but it was definitely Jesse. Or Patrick?

"I know you must be really confused right now," Patrick started.

"Who are you and why did you pull this whole scam on me?" she shouted angrily. Patrick tilted his head in confusion.

"Scam? I never tried to scam you, Jill. Just let me explain..."

"So who are you? Patrick or Jesse or some other name?"

"I'm Patrick Jesse Scott. I go by Patrick now because of my past..."

"And so you knew all along who I was?"

"Yes, but..."

"Oh my gosh! I can't believe I fell for this. You came here to use your charms to get me to give up my property, and I fell for it!" She paced back and forth, throwing her hands in the air occasionally for effect.

"Jill, you've got this all wrong..."

She walked back to him and pointed her finger in his face. "I can't believe you, of all people, are going to tear this bridge down! You know what happened here. I've spent fifteen years thinking about that day and the feelings I had for you after that. I mean, I built you up in my mind like you were some kind of a hero, and boy was I wrong!"

"I'm not a hero, Jill."

"Well, at least we agree on something!" she said as she started walking off the bridge like some kind of speed walking champion.

"I was kidnapped," he said loudly. Jill stopped in her tracks.

She turned and looked at him. "What?"

"I told you my mom and step dad died within a few months of each other, right?"

Jill took a few steps toward him. "Yes."

"Well, I didn't tell you that my biological father, who was a very bad man, kidnapped me after they died."

"I had no idea," Jill said softly.

Patrick turned and looked at the mountains. "After my mom and step dad died, I got kicked into foster care. I was bounced around for over a year. Then, my bio dad appears out of nowhere one day outside of my school. I knew how dangerous he was. He used to beat on my Mom when I was young. We had run away from him, and that's when she met my step dad. He was a good man. I loved him. Anyway, after my Mom died of cancer, my step dad just couldn't handle it. He started drinking and... other things... and he overdosed."

"I'm so sorry, Patrick..." Jill said as she continued walking closer.

"So, anyway, my bio dad shows up at school and basically lures me into the car, promising to take me to buy some new school clothes. Says he's got a great job now and a fancy house. Tells me he wants to make up for everything. Next thing I know, he gives me a soda. I didn't know he'd drugged it, and I wake up here, in the woods, in a tent."

"Oh my gosh..."

"For three months, we lived out here. I couldn't get away. He had weapons, and he made threats... I still don't know why he even took me. He never wanted me. But he was a possessive man, and I guess he thought I was his possession."

"So, how did you end up on the bridge?"

"One morning, we were out hiking and he found someone's old campsite. They'd left a cooler behind, an accident I'm sure, and there was liquor in it. Like a whole bottle of rum or something. He took it back to our campsite and downed the whole thing. Got drunk as a skunk and passed out. It was my chance to finally escape. But, as I was running away, heading to the main road out there, I saw you on the bridge."

"Oh, Patrick..."

He turned to her. "There was something about you, even from a distance. I couldn't leave you behind. It felt like a magnet was drawing me up here."

"So, you came to talk to me even though it meant risking your escape?"

"Yes. And I've never regretted it. When I figured out what you were planning, I was terrified. I didn't know what to say or do."

"You did everything perfectly." She stared up at him,

tears in her eyes. "What happened after you left me that day?"

"It's not important," he said, turning back to the mountains. She could see him clenching his jaw, the muscles twitching under the pressure.

"Patrick, please tell me."

"He caught me about two hundred feet from the road."

"Oh no..." Now the tears were streaming down her face. "What did he do?"

"Let's just say it got physical. I was a strong kid, but my father was six foot three and a former boxer, so I didn't buck him."

"And he kept you here?"

"For six more weeks. Luckily, he slipped up one morning and went fishing before I woke up. He thought I was asleep, but I was faking it. I managed to make it to town and report it to the police. They caught him two days later trying to catch a bus across the country."

"He went to jail?"

"Yes. Spent a few years there, died about six years ago from what I've heard."

"I'm so sorry that I kept you from escaping that day, Patrick."

He turned back to her and smiled. "I'm not sorry at all, Jill."

"But you could've made it to safety if I hadn't been up on this bridge. No wonder you want to tear it down."

"Tear it down? I've never wanted to tear this bridge down!"

Jill's mouth dropped open. "But I heard you talking to Derrick..."

"Yes, he wanted me to do that, but I took him outside to

have a heated conversation about it. I've worked hard for the privilege of making my own decisions, Jill."

"I'm sorry that I doubted you, Patrick. I should've talked to you instead of just believing what I wanted to believe. Gosh, I feel like a complete idiot. Thank you for saving this place. It feels good to know that it will still be here even after you develop this land."

He turned back to her and took both of her hands. "No one is developing this land."

"What?"

"I came back here to tell you two things."

"Okay..."

"For one, I backed out of the conference center deal, but not before buying up the land to protect it. I paid off my partners enough to keep them happy enough to work with me on another project."

"What? Why?"

"Because this place is far too beautiful to be cleared and ruined by 'progress'."

"But what about The Retreat?"

"I bought it from the bank this morning."

"Oh."

Patrick smiled as he pulled an envelope from his back pocket and handed it to her.

"What is this?"

"The deed to your land, including The Retreat and this bridge we're standing on."

"What? Oh, Patrick, I can't accept this..." she started to say.

He laughed. "You can, and you will. I don't want anyone to ever be able to take this place from you. Your focus should be on helping people. Consider this my contribution to humanity."

RACHEL HANNA

She smiled. "I don't know what to say…"

"Say you'll keep doing what you're doing."

"I will. I can't thank you enough."

"No thanks needed. Oh, one more thing… Winston is moving into the guest cottage permanently. He's family, and he really wants to be close to you. Hope that's okay?"

She giggled. "It's more than okay. Wait, you said you had two things to tell me?"

He cleared his throat and rubbed his thumb across her cheek. "The second thing I have to tell you is that I love you, Jill Russell. I've loved you since I saw you on this bridge, and I love you more now. And it's literally the most terrifying thing I've ever said in my life."

Her eyes grew as wide as saucers as she listened to him. "You love me?"

"Yes, and it's okay if you don't feel the same. I just couldn't go on without telling you…"

"Patrick?"

"Yes?"

"I love you too. Now, can we finish that kiss we started all those years ago?"

He smiled broadly. "I thought you'd never ask!"

With that, he pulled her into a tight embrace and pressed his lips to hers. Jill finally understood what a "full circle moment" felt like.

EPILOGUE

Two years later

Jill stood there, staring out over the vast Blue Ridge Mountains, counting her blessings one by one from the last couple of years. Of course, those blessings came out of failure and sadness for a time. After all, Patrick reappeared in her life due to her finances falling apart. If her business had flourished, she might never have seen him again. God knew what he was doing; she believed that with all her heart.

The last twenty-four months had sure been a whirlwind. With Patrick's help, she had been able to pump new life into her business, attracting clients from all over the country to come to her oasis in the mountains. So many stories of healing had come out of the new and improved Retreat, and she was so proud of the work she got to do everyday.

They'd built a large gazebo that served as a chapel for couples wanting to get married at the bridge. They'd already had two weddings there with more scheduled.

Having Winston around everyday had given her back a sense of family, and that was something she sorely needed.

But the thing she was most thankful for in the world was Patrick. He was like a blessing from heaven that she got twice in her life, both at times when she needed him most.

After six months of dating - and helping her revamp her business into something successful - he'd popped the question right there on the bridge. It was perfect. A few months later, they'd had their wedding right in the same spot with Winston, Alice and Ingrid all in attendance.

For a moment, on her wedding day, Jill had thought about her mother and sister, wishing that their relationships could be saved. But there was nothing there to salvage. Patrick had said something to her that made it feel better on the night before their wedding.

"Sweetie," he'd said, "people can't give you what they don't have."

And she realized that nothing was wrong with her, that she wasn't unlovable. It was just that her mother didn't have that required piece of her heart that was meant for mothering. It just wasn't there. And then she felt a little sorry for her sister because she knew that she'd only been brainwashed by a woman who probably wasn't a very good mother to her either, if she would admit it.

Jill had also learned that family wasn't about blood. Anyone could share DNA. But family was about surrounding yourself with people who would be there no matter how dicey life got. She was blessed to have so many of those people around her.

Patrick had moved his business to The Retreat, creating a home office space that allowed him to do everything he did in the city. Of course, he kept his penthouse so he could whisk his wife away a couple of times a month for fun in the city.

"Hey there, sexy lady. Mind if I join you?" Patrick said as

he walked up behind her and slid his arms around her waist. She smiled as she thought about their history together on this bridge. This was the place where she'd planned to end her young life, but in reality it had saved her life that day.

"Well, hello," she said, smiling as she pressed her head back against his chest. "Did the new guests arrive?"

"They did."

"How many?"

"Eight."

Jill turned around and faced him, her eyes wide. "Eight?"

"Yep. It's an entire management team from a company in Florida. They love this place so far and are eagerly looking forward to your yoga class with them this afternoon."

Jill smiled. "I can't believe how fast we're growing."

He ran his finger across her cheek as he cradled her chin in the palm of his hand. "I can. You're an amazing healer and a pretty spectacular wife, if I do say so myself."

She laughed. "You're a little partial, but that's okay. Our growth is only going to get faster as the year goes on."

"I love your optimism!" he said with a chuckle.

Jill stepped back and pulled something from the back pocket of her jeans. "No, I mean I am *positive* we will have a lot of *growth* this year."

It took Patrick a moment of looking back and forth between her and the long plastic stick she had in her hand before he fully caught on. For a billionaire, he wasn't always the quickest when it came to things like this.

"Wait. You're pregnant? We're going to have a baby?" he said, excitement filling his voice as he ran both of his hands through his hair.

"You're going to be a daddy!"

He closed the distance between them and picked her up, twirling her around right there in the middle of the place they first met.

When he finally put her down, he looked at her and smiled. "I have the perfect name if it's a girl."

"Oh yeah? What's that?"

"Bridget. Get it?"

Jill rolled her eyes and laughed. "We'll talk."

Want to read more books by Rachel Hanna? Head over to Amazon to check out these other great books!

The January Cove series:
    The One For Me
    Loving Tessa
    Falling For You
    Finding Love
    All I Need
    Secrets And Soulmates
    Sweet Love
    Choices of the Heart
    Faith, Hope & Love
    Spying On The Billionaire
    Second Chance Christmas

The Whiskey Ridge Series
    Starting Over
    Taking Chances

Home Again
Always A Bridesmaid
The Billionaire's Retreat

Made in the USA
Monee, IL
01 November 2023

45541302R10080